The Loser Dies . . .

Buddy and Will held their positions. Buddy tried to force more speed out of the Cataluna. But the car had reached its limit.

Spin the wheel, Buddy suddenly thought. *A little nudge—and Will crashes and burns!*

Nothing hurts this car. There won't be a scratch.

"Do it," a voice inside his head urged.

Buddy only had seconds to win.

"Do it. Do it."

Seconds to beat Will.

"Do it! Turn the wheel. Give Will a little bump. Make him crash."

Books by R. L. Stine

FEAR STREET®
R·L·STINE

THE CATALUNA CHRONICLES
The Deadly Fire

A Parachute Press Book

AN ARCHWAY PAPERBACK
Published by POCKET BOOKS
New York   London   Toronto   Sydney   Tokyo   Singapore

AN ARCHWAY PAPERBACK *Original*

An Archway Paperback published by
POCKET BOOKS, a division of Simon & Schuster Inc.
1230 Avenue of the Americas, New York, NY 10020

ISBN: 0-671-89435-8

First Archway Paperback printing October 1995

10 9 8 7 6 5 4 3 2 1

FEAR STREET is a registered trademark of Parachute Press, Inc.

AN ARCHWAY PAPERBACK and colophon are registered trademarks of Simon & Schuster Inc.

Cover art by Don Brautigam

Printed in the U.S.A.

IL 7+

The Deadly Fire

prologue

As they stepped out of the movie theater, Chuck Draper slid his arm around his girlfriend Barbara's shoulder. "Cool movie," he said softly.

Barbara Thornton nodded and tossed back her long auburn hair. "Brad Pitt is great!"

Chuck grinned. "I think I look a little bit like him. Don't you?"

Barbara gave him a playful shove, nearly pushing him into their friends Eddie Weiss and Debbie Fielder. "In your dreams!"

Chuck pouted and pretended to be hurt. He glanced up and saw that Eddie and Debbie were having an argument. Again. What is their problem? he wondered. They're always fighting. Why do they keep hanging out together?

"You're just so lame," Debbie was saying.

Eddie defended himself. "People laughed."

"Shouting out dumb remarks in a movie theater is just so lame," Debbie complained. "I was embarrassed. Really. And those guys in front of us were getting really steamed."

"Hey—it was a boring movie, okay?" Eddie grumbled. "I had to do something to keep from falling asleep."

"Making kissing noises during the love scenes is so babyish," Debbie told him.

"You know what your problem is? You have no sense of humor."

They were crossing the Division Street Mall parking lot now, a full moon high in the purple night sky. Chuck knew he had to do something before their argument became a full-scale war.

"Wow. Check out that car!" he declared. He gave a low whistle, then flashed a secret wink at Barbara. They both knew that nothing could distract Eddie faster than a hot car.

"Whoa." Eddie hurried over to the car. "Awesome car!" he cried, running his hand over the insignia on the fender. "A Cataluna? I've never even heard of it."

The white sports car gleamed under the lights of the parking lot. "Check it out!" Eddie exclaimed. "I think I've found my dream car."

Chuck joined his friend beside the car. Debbie and Barbara hung back, talking quietly. Chuck could hear Debbie complaining about Eddie.

"Eddie, the keys are inside!" Chuck announced.

"Huh? You kidding me?" Eddie bent down and peered through the passenger window.

Chuck slid his hand along the driver's door. The metal felt warm. He felt a slight vibration running through it. "I don't believe this. It's running. The motor's running."

"Whoa. That's crazy. Nobody could walk off and leave a car like this with the motor running," Eddie protested.

"Sure they could. It runs so quietly," Chuck replied. "Say the guy is late for a movie. He grabs the first spot he comes to, then jumps out and runs inside."

Barbara and Debbie wandered over. "Maybe we should turn it off for them," Debbie suggested.

"Yeah, we will," Chuck agreed. He opened the driver's door and slid in behind the wheel. He turned to the others and grinned. "As soon as we get back."

"Yes!" Eddie cried. He grabbed Debbie's hand and tried to pull her into the backseat.

"No way!" she cried. "You guys took a car last week and—"

"Borrowed it!" Eddie corrected her with a grin.

"And we almost got caught. No way I'm coming with you tonight."

"We'll just take it for five minutes," Chuck argued. "The guy is in the movie theater, right? And the late show just started. We'll have a five-minute test-drive and bring the car right back to this spot."

The two girls protested for a bit, but eventually gave in and climbed into the low, white car. "Five minutes. You promised," Debbie told Chuck, checking her watch.

Chuck didn't reply. He was concentrating on the sleek dashboard, trying to locate the switch for the lights. A few seconds later he pulled the car out of the lot. "We'll take it around the block. Okay?" He glanced at Barbara beside him. "Don't look so tense. I'll have it back here in two minutes."

Maybe a few blocks, he thought. Yeah, a couple of blocks, tops.

The wheel felt as if it had been designed for him. The seat fit him perfectly. His right leg connected smoothly with the gas pedal.

"I just want to see what it'll do," he announced, pulling onto the deserted Mill Road.

"Come on, Chuck. You promised—!" Debbie pleaded.

"Yeah. Turn it around," Barbara insisted. "Now!"

He didn't hear them. He felt himself becoming one with the car. I could drive this baby all night, he thought. So smooth. So fast.

"Chuck, turn the radio down a little." Debbie's shrill voice from the backseat.

Chuck hadn't noticed it was on. His hand fumbled for the radio knob. He twisted it.

The music got louder. A girl singing.

"Wrong way!" Barbara complained. She reached out and turned the knob in the opposite direction.

The music got even louder.

"Turn it off!" Debbie shouted over the music. "We don't want to attract attention. You're going to have the police after us!"

"Yeah, man. Shut it down!" Eddie agreed, holding his ears.

Chuck twisted the knob again.

The music blared louder.

"Turn it off, turn it off, turn it off!" Debbie shrieked. Chuck could barely hear her over the deafening music.

"I can't turn it off!" Chuck screamed.

He swerved the car to the side of the road and screeched to a stop. The music hammered at them. Chuck wanted to cover his ears. But he needed one hand to try to turn off the music.

Louder.

"Ow! It hurts! It hurts so much!" Debbie wailed, pressing her hands against her ears.

"Cut the engine!" Eddie pleaded from the backseat. "Cut the engine!"

Chuck shoved the car into Park and turned off the ignition.

The music blasted out even louder.

His ears began to ache. His temples throbbed. He felt his stomach tighten as a wave of nausea swept over him.

"Stop it! Stop it!" Debbie shrieked, pounding the radio with both fists.

Her frantic efforts made the music louder. No longer music, but a painful, grating roar.

"Out! Let's get out!" Chuck cried.

Hands grabbed the door handles. Tugged hard.

"The door won't open!"

"We're locked in!"

Louder. The music roared as if it had invaded their heads, inside them now.

A sharp stab of pain shot through Chuck's head.

He felt wetness, warm wetness on the sides of his face. His hands shot up to his ears. When he pulled them away, they were covered with blood.

My eardrums. My eardrums exploded. The deafening sound—it burst my eardrums!

But still the music roared, louder, louder.

Trembling in fear and horror, he raised his hands again. Felt the hot blood spurting out of his ears.

Louder. Louder.

He turned to Barbara. Saw her twisting in agony. Blood pouring down the sides of her tear-stained face. She struggled with the door handle, tugging, jerking. But the car door didn't budge.

He turned to see Eddie and Debbie, desperately struggling to free themselves. Blood spurted from their ears. Their eyes were wild with terror.

6

Louder. Louder.

Then silence filled the car. Silence for all four of them.

Silence forever.

Four more victims for me. Or perhaps I should say, four more victims for the Cataluna, the Car of Doom.

I have to laugh. If I didn't, I would cry and cry and never stop. I was a living, breathing girl once—before my spirit became trapped in this white car. But that was long ago. I lived in another century and another place.

In the year 1698, I was sixteen. A girl of the West Hampshire Colony. People were superstitious then. They saw the red crescent birthmark on my forehead and said I had been born under a bad moon.

I did not learn the real truth about myself until I discovered my true mother. She was also born under a bad moon, but one that shone in the twentieth century, one that blessed her with powerful, dark magic. My mother could change her shape, become a cat, a mouse, any creature she desired.

The people of the 1990s tormented her. They called her insane. They would have locked her away simply for being different.

So my mother used her magic to escape. In the sleek white car she traveled back in time three hundred years. She landed in the West Hampshire Colony.

I was born there—born under the same bad moon. I suffered the same fate as my mother. The people of the colony hated me because I was different. I had done no one harm, but the people blamed me for all their bad luck. They called me evil.

And finally I proved them right.

I murdered—and enjoyed it.

But what choice did I have? The people of the colony killed my mother. Then they came to hang me.

My dead mother's voice guided me to the white car. I used its magic to escape. The car carried me to the twentieth century. To a town called Shadyside.

But my enemy came along. Yes, I had made an enemy in the West Hampshire Colony. William Parker.

I had murdered William's brother. Murdered his father. They deserved to die.

But William came after me, seeking revenge. He vowed to follow me wherever I went. To find me. To destroy me.

He jumped into the back of the white car as it carried me forward to my mother's time—three hundred years into my future.

The car crashed. I died. William died.

But my spirit somehow escaped my crushed body. To my horror, it became locked in the sleek, white car. My mind remained my mind. But but my body had been replaced by steel and glass and rubber.

And what of William?

The question haunts me. Did William's spirit survive as well? Is he also alive in some other form, some other body?

Is he searching for me, still thirsting to destroy me?

Yes. I know the answer must be yes.

William will never stop hunting for me.

I decided to stay alert. To act first. To destroy anyone who came near me.

I have no choice. Even as a car, I want to live.

Because I choose to protect myself, I am known as the Doom Car. But I don't care what they call me. I *will* mean doom for William Parker.

If he dares come after me.

part

1

chapter

1

*B*uddy McCloy kissed Sara Franklin again. This time on the nose. He would eventually kiss her on the mouth, but not yet. He loved to tease her this way—kissing her ear, her cheek, her forehead—working his way around her face until he finally reached her lips.

Buddy's oldest brother, Stan, had taught him the trick, promising that all girls loved it. Stan had agreed to teach Buddy a few more tricks when he got "old enough to handle them."

"Hey, runt," came a voice out of nowhere. "Break it up."

Buddy and Sara broke apart. Buddy's brother Sean tossed their jackets at them.

"Hey, give a guy a break," Buddy protested. Sean wasn't nearly as cool as Stan. His mother used to say it was strange that three boys could appear so much alike—all handsome, with brown hair and brown eyes—and act so differently.

"No chance," Sean called, heading for the front door. "We've got twenty minutes to get down to Waynesbridge. Stan's driving in the first event. In the Doom Car."

Buddy shot up off the couch, pulling Sara behind him. "Dad's going to let Stan drive the Cataluna today?"

"Yeah. Where have you been? They've been dog-blunting the car all week."

"I know that," Buddy answered as he shrugged on his coat. He didn't have to tell Sara to hurry. She already had her jacket on. Sara never missed a chance to hang out at the speedway, especially with someone who could get her out of the stands and down in the pits.

Sometimes Buddy wondered if Sara liked him—or the fact that he was one of the McCloys. Everyone at the racetrack knew Buddy's family. Buddy's dad had been a driver. Then, when Buddy's mother died, Mr. McCloy had stopped racing and opened a body shop. Stan, Sean, and Buddy had all picked up his love of racing.

Buddy and Sara hurried out the door, trying to catch up to Sean. "What's 'dog-blunting'?" Sara asked.

"I don't know . . . working on the motor, I guess," Buddy replied.

Sean liked to talk with every driver, off-roader, and ratchet jockey he could find. He picked up new phrases and abandoned them so quickly that the rest of his family had grown to ignore him. "Listen carefully and hope for the best," their father always advised Buddy and Stan.

By the time Buddy locked the front door, Sean had backed his Chevy S-10 out from behind the house. Buddy and Sara ran across the front lawn and jumped down from the built-up yard into the bed of the truck. Sean pulled out onto Park Drive.

"I don't get it!" Sara shouted, hanging on to the roll bar as Sean took a wild turn onto Hawthorne. Her strawberry-blond hair blew into her face. "How come you didn't know about Stan racing today?"

Sean stopped at a red light and revved the engine. "Must have just happened," Buddy told her. "Someone down at Waynesbridge probably offered Dad big bucks to bring the Doom Car out today as a last-minute sub."

The light changed and Sean spun around the corner. Buddy banged on the back window, but Sean didn't turn around. Sean got a kick out of tossing around passengers riding in the truck bed.

Dad was right, Buddy thought. The Cataluna's bad reputation is a great gimmick. His father had bought the car *because* of the rumors that it had killed a dozen people.

Mr. McCloy didn't believe the stories himself. How could they be true? he'd asked Buddy. The car doesn't have a mark on it.

But Mr. McCloy knew that the stories sold tickets. Everyone wanted to watch the evil Doom Car go around the track.

"This is so cool!" Sara shouted as Sean roared into the Waynesbridge Speedway. He zoomed straight for Gasoline Alley, the infield garage area the racers used for repairs and refueling. Then he squealed to a stop.

"I didn't know *you* were racing today, Sean!" Mr. McCloy joked, running up to the truck.

"Come on, Dad," Sean protested, leaping out of the passenger side. The driver's side had ended up too close to his father's Jeep for him to open the door. "No way could we miss the Torque Master launch out in the Deathmobile."

"Hello, Sara," Mr. McCloy said as Buddy and his girlfriend clambered down from the truck bed.

Sara waved. "Can I check out the Doom Car?" she asked, her green eyes sparkling with excitement.

Sara eagerly hurried over to the gleaming white car. Mr. McCloy looped his arm around Buddy's shoulders. "At least now I know why you were too busy to answer the phone earlier," he said softly.

"Sorry, Dad," Buddy replied. "Why the quick entry today?"

"Jake Thompson got held up somewhere on the road down from Oregon. Some nonsense about his girlfriend's cat getting out of the trailer and him having to stay there and search for it."

Buddy stared at his father. Missing a race over a lost cat? He couldn't believe it.

Hey, he thought, if it gives the Cataluna a shot, who cares?

"How much money did they put up, Dad?"

"Plenty," answered Mr. McCloy, flashing his son a big smile. "Two thousand to show up and let people gawk at her. Two thousand to actually take her out on the track, and five thousand more as a late-call fee."

Whoa, Buddy thought. In one day his father had recouped almost half his initial investment. The Doom Car sure wasn't bringing the McCloys any bad luck.

"And, of course, if Stan takes today's purse—" his father continued.

"Hey, where is Stan anyway?" Buddy interrupted.

"Right here, Gilhooley."

Stan broke away from a group of drivers back by the gas pumps. Buddy trotted over to him.

"Smile when you say that," Buddy joked. He would never forget the day his brother had given him the nickname Gilhooley.

Buddy's first time driving a dirt-track machine, he misjudged a turn. He ended up in a violent, track-tearing spin and lost all control of the car. Stan's car.

Stan didn't say a word about the car. "Nice gilhooley," he called, using the dirt circuit term for a

17

spinout. The nickname stuck—although Buddy wouldn't let anyone but his big brother use it.

Buddy punched his brother on the arm. "You'd better get moving. They're calling for the flag."

Stan strapped on his helmet and slapped his brother on the back. "Yes, *Pappy*. Whatever you say."

Buddy followed Stan to the white car. He could feel the eyes of all the people in the speedway on the two of them. Everyone in Shadyside had heard of the Doom Car. Now they were going to get to see it race for the first time.

As Stan belted himself into the Cataluna, Buddy joined Sara near the driver's-side window. He had never really liked the car. Not from the day his father bought it. Buddy couldn't say why—he wasn't afraid of it, didn't really think it killed people on its own. But he found himself avoiding the car.

Buddy shoved the dark thoughts out of his mind. He grabbed his brother's hand in the secret shake they had shared since they were kids. He didn't let go at the end.

Stan stared up at his brother. "What?" he asked when Buddy kept gripping his hand.

"Hey, Stan—you be careful in this thing. Like . . . uh . . . good luck, you know?"

"Luck has nothing to do with it, Gilhooley." Stan broke the handshake. "The stories about this car are all hype. A car is just a car."

Stan flashed Buddy the V sign with his left hand,

firing the ignition with his right. Buddy backed away from the car and Sara grabbed his hand. Together they walked back toward the others.

Buddy glanced back at the sleek white Cataluna. Stan is right, he told himself. A car is just a car. So why do I have such a bad feeling about this race?

chapter

2

Stan stared out at the crowd, gripping the wheel as he waited for the race to begin. He knew what the people in the stands were thinking.

I wonder if the Doom Car will kill someone today. I wonder if I'll see someone die.

"Sorry to disappoint you folks," Stan joked to himself, using a deep announcer's voice. "We have no scheduled crashes on the program today."

But Stan couldn't help remembering Buddy's tense expression. Or the worry in his brother's voice when he said, "You be careful in this thing."

Stop, Stan ordered himself. You're getting nuts. The Cataluna is a hunk of metal and rubber. You and Dad worked on every inch. The car will perform.

His father's advice rang in his ears. "Don't bleed off all your energy before the race. Think about other stuff—anything—and hold back. Learn to wait until you see that the time man is all set up and waiting for the flag. Then let it build. Let that heat start turning over in your belly."

Stan's eyes focused on the clocker and the flag man.

Time man's set, Dad, he thought. He gripped the ivory white ball of the stick shift in his right hand.

Flag is on the track. Stan's eyes darted around an invisible five-point circle. Rearview mirror—flagman—right-side mirror—left-side mirror—car in front. Rearview mirror—flagman—right-side mirror—left-side mirror—car in front . . .

The flag fell.

The car ahead of Stan jumped two feet in front of the others in the first row. Stan stayed on its tail, not losing an inch.

He hugged its rear bumper the whole way to the first turn. As they tore around it, Stan grabbed a chance to pull in front of the other car.

Yes! Second row into first row before the first half lap, Stan thought. That's the way to do it.

Stan glanced in his rearview mirror. Don't even think about trying to pass me. No one can beat Stan McCloy and the Doom Car! He took the track's first turn again, passing cars from the rows just entering the race.

Hunching down behind the wheel, Stan kept his eyes moving. They darted back and forth constantly, searching for holes opening ahead of him and cars trying to move up from behind.

Around the fifteenth lap he let his eyes start skimming the crowd too, watching for rises or falls in their excitement level. People usually drifted over to the concession stands at this point in the race. Or settled into their seats and talked to friends.

But Stan could tell the crowd was still with him. People hung over the rails, waving wildly. They stood in the stands, cheering and yelling.

They're cheering for me, Stan realized. Me and the Doom Car. They thought this baby was a novelty. Something to give them a thrill. But we're in the top three! The top *three!*

Stan patted the dashboard affectionately. "You're bad luck all right, girl. Bad luck to anyone else who wants to win this race."

Coming off the far turn, Stan shifted through the gears, flooring the gas. A straight line opened up, four solid car lengths long. He spotted another hole about to open to the left. Within seconds Stan pulled another eight car-lengths ahead.

Immediately his eyes began hunting for another spot to swing into before he had to downshift. Lose speed—lose a place. And I'm not out to lose, Stan thought.

A Dodge on his right fell back half a length. Stan grabbed the space in front of it. Lunging for the forward position meant moving to the outside rail, but Stan didn't care. I'll make it up on the turn, he thought.

A girl laughed.

Where did that come from? Stan thought. The radio? No, Dad and I disconnected it weeks ago.

Five cars edged past the Cataluna. Stan fought to hold his ground.

How did I hear that voice over the noise of the race? Stan wondered.

Distracted, he missed a break in the wall of cars to his left. Oh, great, he thought. Now I'm trapped in the outer ring until the far turn. Unless . . .

A wedge of five cars fought for position just ahead of him. The leader would break to the right—Stan knew it, could see it coming. If he forced his way up behind the leader, he could take the wedge's nose position and break free.

Stan wrenched the steering wheel to the left and then the right. The Cataluna swung over far enough to intimidate the driver of the next car—without touching the car itself.

The driver to his left hesitated, afraid to connect with the "killer car." Stan grabbed his spot and slid behind the lead car. The leader moved into the hole opening on the right.

Got it! Stan thought. He ran through the gears, giving the Cataluna as much gas as it could take.

The laughter invaded his ears again. A girl's laughter. Low and teasing.

"Where is it coming from?" Stan yelled.

Who cares? answered a voice in the back of his head. You've got a race to win. Everyone is counting on you. All that matters is first place and the gate purse.

Crouching behind the wheel, Stan ignored the laughter. But it grew louder and louder, closer.

Stan threw all his concentration into the race. Maintaining his pressure on the gas pedal, he took advantage of the wide stretch of open track.

The turn approached fast. Stan dropped his hand to the stick shift, ready to down gear. He let up on the gas slightly and pulled back on the ivory ball, planning to shift into third gear.

The girl's laughter swelled.

The stick shift did not move.

"Huh?"

Shock sent a cold shiver through Stan's body.

Only seconds before he reached the turn. Desperately he yanked on the stick. Frozen. It wouldn't budge.

The laughter rang in his helmet. Stan hit the brake with his left foot. The pedal didn't move. He slammed his foot down violently, but the brake pedal would not budge.

Stan tore at the steering wheel. It also locked in place.

He frantically jammed both feet down on the brake. Jerked back the stick shift with one hand. Yanked on the wheel with the other.

The Cataluna raced straight toward the guardrail.

He heard metal crash against metal. He saw sparks fly into the air.

Stan's head slammed hard into the steering wheel, then bounced back against the seat.

The Doom Car smashed through the guardrail and plowed through the hay barrier.

The white car slammed up over the restraining wall.

Stan's vision blurred. He fought to focus. A shrill wail of terror escaped his throat.

The Cataluna crashed into the bleachers. People scrambled to escape, their mouths wide in horrified screams.

Through the crowded bleachers. Into the concrete power station behind the grandstand.

Stan's head snapped forward again. His helmet shattered against the wheel. The sharp fiberglass fragments tore open his forehead. Long slivers drove their way into his skull.

Electricity shot through the car—through his body.

The last sounds Stan heard were the screams of the dying people in the stands behind him. His own howls of pain.

And the girl's taunting laughter in his ear.

chapter

3

Goodbye, Stan. Or should I call you William?

Have I finally destroyed you, William Parker? Or did you escape again, into the body of one of the other McCloys? Do I have to kill them all to get you?

Don't worry, William. I would not think of playing favorites. I will give them all their chance—and I will get you in the end. Wherever you go, wherever you hide. Don't you know that you never really get rid of the moon?

It only seems to disappear, but it always comes back.

Always.

* * *

Buddy sat on the couch in his dark living room. The only light came from the TV. He ran through the forty-three available channels.

CLICK ... "Top Cat" ... CLICK ... "Designing Women" ... CLICK ... evening news ... CLICK ... nature film ... CLICK ... sci-fi movie ... CLICK ... "Gilligan's Island" ... CLICK ... CLICK ... CLICK ... CLICK ... Thirty-three more tries only brought him back around to "Top Cat."

Buddy shut off the TV and let the clicker fall to the floor. He didn't want to watch TV. He didn't want to do anything. If Stan could die doing what he did best, what was the point?

Buddy stared out the window. But all he could see was the Cataluna crashing through the guardrail.

It's not fair, he thought. It's not fair. I still can't believe it. What happened? How could Stan have lost control like that? He was so good. He was the best.

I don't understand anything about it. The car survives without a scratch—without a scratch!—and Stan dies. Electrocuted. Shock after shock. And the upholstery didn't even get scorched.

Buddy felt sick to his stomach. He'd felt sick every day of the two weeks since Stan died.

People blamed his family for the six people killed in the bleachers. They said Mr. McCloy never should have raced the Doom Car. He knew it was a killer, and now it had killed again.

Buddy knew the whispers and accusations tore at

his father. And Buddy knew his father blamed himself for Stan's death.

After all, Mr. McCloy bought the Cataluna, worked on it with Stan, arranged their spot in the race, put Stan in the driver's seat.

Now the car remained and Stan was gone. Mr. McCloy spent most of his time searching for a buyer for the Cataluna. No one wanted to talk about it. No one even wanted to think about it.

I don't want to think about it, either. Buddy checked his watch. After seven.

Where is Sara? She promised she would be here by five-thirty. How are we supposed to get something to eat before the party if she's so late?

Buddy grabbed the phone. He punched in Sara's number, shoving each button down hard. When the second ring came and no one picked up, he knew she wasn't home. Sara always tore through the house when the phone rang.

The phone rang four more times. Definitely not home. Buddy let the phone keep ringing.

So where is she? Is she: A) on her way, B) making me wait because she's at the mall hanging out with her friends, or C) standing me up—for the second time this week?

Eight rings, nine rings . . .

"Hello." Sara's mother. Breathless.

"Hello, Mrs. Franklin. Is Sara there?"

"Oh, hello, Buddy. Is that you?"

Of course it's me, Buddy wanted to yell. It's always me. We do this every single time I call.

"Yes, Mrs. Franklin. Is Sara there?"

"No, Buddy. She went out—oh, quite a while ago. She told me she was going to a party. In fact, I thought she said she was going with you."

"Yeah. We were going to a party." Buddy didn't mention when they were supposed to meet. He didn't want to get Sara in any trouble. "I wanted to make sure she remembered."

"Oh, but I wonder—"

"She must have hooked up with Lisa and Mollie." Buddy cut Mrs. Franklin off before she could begin to speculate on Sara's whereabouts. "They probably stopped at the mall on their way here."

"Well, as long as you're not worried." Mrs. Franklin hesitated. Buddy knew what came next. He had been enduring it from everyone for two weeks. Finally she said, "I haven't seen you for a while. I hope everything's all right."

"I'm fine, Mrs. Franklin."

"We all feel so bad about your brother," she continued.

"Thank you."

Buddy hung up the phone. If he had to answer one more card, or talk to one more relative, or get stopped in the hall at school by one more person . . .

"Stan's dead!" he shouted. He picked up the sofa pillow next to him and hurled it across the room. "Why can't people shut up about it?"

Sean walked in at that moment, getting the pillow square in the chest. "Calm down, runt."

"Make me, gear head."

"Whoa, don't make me teach you some manners," Sean teased.

"Don't try it. I'm not in the mood to take anything off you today. Understand?" Buddy glared at his brother.

"Yeah, I understand. Stan was my brother, too, you know." Sean crossed over to the couch and dropped the pillow next to Buddy.

"Sara stood you up again, huh?" Sean asked.

"Do me a favor, will 'ya? Drop dead."

"Don't give *me* a hard time. Sara's the one messing with you."

"Shut up, Sean."

"I'm telling you this for your own good. You're nuts about her and she's using it to her advantage. You're getting way too serious about her."

Buddy turned away from his brother. Maybe Sean would take the hint and go away.

He didn't. He plopped down on the sofa next to Buddy. "Maybe you should cool it with Sara for a while," Sean suggested.

Buddy didn't want advice from Sean. When he needed help, he always talked to Stan. Stan didn't treat him like a little kid.

But Stan was dead.

Buddy turned back to face Sean. "I can live without your advice—all right?" he yelled. You're only ten months older than me, anyway. What makes you think you're so wise?"

"Maybe I've seen a little more than you have. I think you are a lot more serious than Sara is—and you're going to end up getting hurt."

"Hey, I'll take my chances." Buddy grabbed his jacket from the arm of the couch and stormed across the room. At the kitchen door he turned and pointed his finger at Sean. "Don't ever talk to me about Sara again."

Buddy rushed through the kitchen and out the back door, slamming it behind him. It crashed against the frame, bounced out, then banged shut again.

Buddy stood on the back porch, staring out at the yard. He didn't know what to do. Should he go to the party? What if Sara was there? What if she went with someone else?

Why aren't you here to tell me what to do, Stan? he thought. Why aren't you here?

Buddy jumped off the porch and strode over to the garage. He threw open the wide swinging doors. *"You're* why Stan isn't here!" he shouted at the Cataluna. "You killed him!"

Buddy stared at the Doom Car. There wasn't a dent or a mark on it. Not a single sign that it had killed seven people two weeks earlier.

"I wish I could pull a switch and crush you down into a salvage block," he muttered.

"Wouldn't it be more fun to go for a drive?

"Get the keys."

The words whispered in his head. He heard them in a soft female voice.

"Go ahead, Buddy. Get the keys.

"Get the keys."

Buddy took a step forward. He knew he could never drive the Cataluna. His father had forbidden it.

"Get the keys, Buddy."

No! The car killed Stan. He hated it. Hated it.

Buddy moved a little closer to the Cataluna.

"Get the keys."

The female voice sounded so close. So close. Right in his ear.

chapter

4

"Hello . . . hello."

The girl's voice sounded so close.

Buddy stumbled backward.

"Careful."

Did the voice come from the car?

No! That's impossible! Buddy spun around.

Instantly he felt like a prize jerk. The voice didn't come from the car—it came from behind him. From one of the most beautiful girls he had ever seen.

And the first thing I do is almost step on her. Great!

Buddy jumped back a step. "Sorry. I didn't hear you. I mean, I heard you, but I didn't know you were there—here. I mean, behind me . . ."

The girl was tall, with medium-length black hair

that moved in waves as she turned her head. She had large brown eyes with long lashes. Longer even than Sara's.

"I'm sorry I scared you," she apologized. "I moved in next door a couple days ago, and, well, I noticed you in your backyard, and I thought—"

"I didn't expect anyone to be back here," he explained. "I wanted to come out and—" Buddy felt his face turning red.

He stopped, not knowing what to say.

How do I tell her I wanted to destroy the Doom Car? And that I thought I heard it talking to me? She'll think I'm totally messed up.

He started again. "I'm Buddy McCloy. You said you just moved in?"

"Yeah," the girl replied shyly. "I'm Marisol Prince. I'm your new neighbor. I guess."

"Hi," he answered, finally smiling.

Weird day, Buddy thought. *Missing Stan. Fighting with Sean. Getting stood up by Sara. And now feeling pretty good talking to this great-looking girl.*

Except I'm not talking, Buddy realized. *I'm standing around like the biggest geek in the universe.*

Buddy saw Marisol eyeing the Cataluna. "You like cars?" he asked.

"I like this one. Is it yours?"

"No, it's my dad's. Well, it's sort of the whole family's, I guess. My dad bought it as an investment," Buddy explained. "He owns a body shop–parts store.

He used to be a racer. But after Mom died he opened a business so he could take care of us kids."

"You have brothers and sisters?" Marisol asked.

"Brothers." Buddy winced, then corrected himself. "I mean a brother." He stared at the garage floor. "I had two, but my brother Stan . . . he died a couple of weeks ago."

"Oh, I'm sorry." Marisol touched his arm, then quickly pulled her hand away. After an awkward silence she admitted, "I know how you feel. I had a brother who died, too."

Buddy realized he didn't mind talking to Marisol about Stan. She wasn't trying to be nice like Mrs. Franklin or the kids at school. Marisol seemed to understand how he felt.

"He died in a race," Buddy told her. He pointed toward the Cataluna. "In this car."

"Oh, wow," Marisol whispered. She stared at the white car. "Wait a minute," she said slowly. "You said your brother died a couple of weeks ago in a race? In this car?"

Buddy nodded.

Marisol pointed at the Cataluna. "This is the car everyone's talking about, isn't it—the Doom Car?"

"Yeah," he answered, his stomach twisting. "This is it."

"Oh, I'm sorry." Marisol shook her head unhappily. "I seem to keep saying the wrong thing to you."

"No, I'm sorry," he told her. "It's not your fault we own this car."

Marisol stepped up to the Cataluna. She ran her fingers over the roof. She seemed fascinated. "I'm surprised it's in such good shape after the wreck."

"Everybody is surprised. It went through a guard-rail, through the bleachers, and then rammed into a power station. Didn't get a dent. Not a scratch. Nothing."

Marisol continued to study the car. She ran her hand over the fender.

"Good thing, I guess," Buddy added with a sigh. "The only thing that kept us from getting sued."

"What do you mean?"

"The police and the insurance investigators are blaming the speedway," Buddy explained. "They said the guardrail and stands must have been loose or defective or something. Otherwise there's no way a car could crash through all that stuff without at least scraping off some paint."

"Wow—it should be on 'Unsolved Mysteries' or something!" Marisol exclaimed.

Buddy agreed. Everyone who inspected the car after the accident had been so quiet—almost fright-ened. Buddy wondered if they could feel something evil when they touched the Cataluna.

"Well, if there was no damage, what is this red spot on the fender?" Marisol asked, interrupting his thoughts. "It's shaped like a crescent moon."

"I know. We thought it was some kind of company logo. Dad checked everywhere for the manufacturer in case we needed spare parts. But he couldn't find one," Buddy explained.

"So what does that mean?" Marisol asked. "That it's a one-of-a-kind?"

"Yeah," Buddy answered. "I guess." He thought the Cataluna had to be some kind of novelty car—a test model made by one of the big companies, or something an inventor put together in his garage. But he didn't want to talk about the car to this beautiful girl.

"Buddy, take me for a ride," Marisol whispered. Her dark eyes flashed excitedly.

"Excuse me?" Buddy exclaimed.

"Let's take it out for a ride—the Cataluna. Oh, please. Could we?"

What am I going to say? Buddy asked himself. Sorry, Marisol. My dad won't let me drive the car because it has a curse on it.

Yeah, right. She'll definitely think I'm messed up.

And I want her to like me. The thought surprised Buddy. He'd spent all of fifteen minutes with Marisol. But, yeah, he really wanted her to like him.

It felt good talking to her, which was more than he could say about Sara lately.

Sara. Buddy checked his watch—almost eight. I've definitely been stood up, he decided. Again.

Maybe a short ride to show off the Cataluna to Marisol, Buddy thought. What could that hurt?

"I'll get the keys," he heard himself tell her. "No problem."

Marisol smiled happily.

"Wait here," Buddy called as he ran back toward the house. A short ride, he thought again. That's all. What could happen?

chapter

5

*B*efore Buddy reached the house, a car turned into his driveway.

"Buddy! Yo, Buddy."

Peter Bailey called to him from his beat-up Honda. He pulled the rust bucket to a stop a few feet from Buddy with George Carman already climbing out through the passenger window.

"Hey, Pete! George!"

"Hey," Pete answered. He revved his shaky engine. "Come on, man, jump in. We've got to get you out of this dump."

Buddy stared, surprised to see his two best friends. They weren't supposed to pick him up. He trotted

39

over to the car. "I thought you guys were going straight to the party."

"We were. We did," Pete answered. "Dull place without you, man."

"Yeah, sure." Buddy recognized the attempt to cheer him up. He wished people would leave him alone. Especially now. He wanted to spend some time with Marisol.

Buddy felt trapped. He leaned down next to Pete. "Is Sara at the party?" He asked as softly as he could over the sounds of the Honda.

"Yeah," Pete told him. "Having a good time, too."

George circled the car, grabbed Buddy around the chest, and shoved him back against the Honda. "Tie him up!" he screamed. "Throw him in the trunk. Hit the gas. We've got to get him out of here! He needs to party!"

"Hey, knock it off," Buddy snapped. "You animal! Can't you ever act like a human being?"

"No way," George answered. "Coach has been feeding me too much red meat."

George was huge, a tackle on the Shadyside High Tigers. He released Buddy. Buddy moved away from the car and straightened his jacket. "Give me a break, man."

"You coming or not?" Pete demanded, thumping the side of the Honda.

Buddy glanced over at the dark-haired girl still standing next to the garage, then back at his friends.

"Wait for me," he told Pete, then hurried over to Marisol.

"I'm sorry." Buddy couldn't quite meet Marisol's eyes. He felt stupid and embarrassed. "I forgot I had this party tonight. I wish I could take you with me, but—"

"That's okay, Buddy," Marisol replied. "I'll catch you later."

Buddy closed the garage. "Yeah. See you around."

Marisol turned away and headed back toward her own yard. Buddy watched her. Even in the darkness he could tell she felt disappointed.

"Come on, man—before my engine falls out in your driveway," Pete yelled.

Buddy jogged over to the car and slid into the backseat, letting George take shotgun. George could barely fit in the front. No way he could fit in the back.

Buddy didn't mind being stuck in the back this time. He had a lot to think about.

"George needs food!" George bellowed when they arrived at Gary Brandt's party. He slammed through the crowd of people as though he were breaking through the defensive line.

Pete cracked up. "If you're hungry, you'd better get over there fast," he advised Buddy.

"No," Buddy mumbled, already scanning the room for Sara.

"Pretty cool, huh!" Pete shouted over the music. "Gary calls it video wallpaper."

Buddy nodded.

Gary had gathered a bunch of TVs and VCRs and spread them all over the basement—with the sound off. Each screen showed something different. "Beavis and Butthead." One of the *Terminator* movies. "Mister Rogers." A dinosaur. An old comedy with Chevy Chase.

Pete grabbed Buddy's arm. "Hey, let's go talk to Meg and Shannon. Check'em out. Over in that corner."

"No. I'm going to get a Coke or something. I'll catch you later."

"You sure?" Pete asked.

Buddy could tell that Pete was worried about him. "I'm sure," Buddy answered, trying not to sound annoyed.

He wandered toward a big plastic garbage can filled with ice and cans of soda. Where is Sara? he wondered. She wouldn't have left yet. She loves parties.

He scanned the room again and caught a glimpse of long strawberry-blond hair. Sara. She sat on the edge of the sofa, laughing at some story of Mollie's.

I'm not going over there, Buddy thought. She stood me up. She should come over to me and apologize.

But what if she doesn't? What if she never comes over?

Buddy fought his way over to the sodas and fished out a Cherry Coke. He popped the top and took a long swallow. Then he stared over at Sara again.

She wasn't talking to Mollie anymore. A guy had taken Mollie's place.

Buddy had never seen him before. He was pale, with blond hair slicked back in a short ponytail, and he wore a long black jacket that came down almost to his knees.

He buy that thing in an antique shop, or what? Buddy thought. That's not going to impress Sara. It's too weird looking.

But as Buddy watched, Sara playfully popped a potato chip into the blond boy's mouth.

She's coming on to him!

Buddy tasted something sour in the back of his throat. First she stands me up. Then she doesn't even bother to apologize. And now Sara is flirting with a weird-looking new guy—right in front of me!

Buddy didn't know what to do. He didn't want to get into an argument at a party. He knew if he started a fight with Sara now, she would win. "Girls always win when you're stuck in a social situation," Stan once told him.

The longer Buddy stared, the angrier he got. He closed his fist around his soda can, crushing it. The Coke shot up out of the hole in the top. It ran over Buddy's hand and onto the floor.

Even though no one noticed what happened, Buddy felt embarrassed. He grabbed some napkins and mopped up the soda.

"Can't take you anywhere," someone called. Buddy

jerked his head up. Gary Brandt grinned at him. "How's it going, man?"

Buddy shrugged. "Okay." He glanced over at Sara again. "Hey, Gary, who's the guy in the black jacket? The one with the ponytail."

Gary shrugged. "I don't know. He came with someone. He's new. I think his name is Will."

"Gary!" Mollie yelled from across the room. "Can we get some different music? I hate this metal junk."

"Got to go." Gary slapped Buddy on the shoulder.

Buddy stared over at Sara again. Now she's practically sitting in that guy Will's lap, he thought. I've got to get out of here before I do something stupid.

Buddy wove through the crowd to the porch. He hung out for a while, but the porch was almost as crowded as the basement. And Buddy didn't feel like talking to anyone.

He wandered around to the backyard. This is even worse, he thought. It's make-out city. Wow. Lots of fun watching other couples when my girlfriend is inside flirting with some strange guy.

I'm outta here, Buddy decided. If Pete and George want to leave, great. If not, I'm walking. Buddy strode quickly to the front of the house.

I should have stayed home. I should have taken Marisol for that ride. I should have taken Marisol for a ride and brought her here. I should have . . .

Buddy climbed up the porch steps fast, head down.

He slammed into someone coming the other way. Buddy started to apologize, then realized he'd run into Will—the guy Sara seemed to be so interested in.

"Hey! Watch it, man," Will snapped. He pushed Buddy, almost knocking him back off the porch.

"Whoa. It was an accident," Buddy protested. He stood at the edge of the porch. He felt his fingers curling into fists.

Kids whispered to one another, watching them, waiting for something to happen.

Buddy held himself back. People have enough bad things to say about the McCloys already, he thought.

He stared Will in the eye. Cold, Buddy thought. This guy is cold.

"I hear you like to race," Will said.

Buddy blinked. "Maybe."

"I hear you own the Doom Car. I hear you and your family think it's pretty fast."

Buddy blinked again. What did this guy want, anyway?

"What's it to you?" Buddy shot back.

"My car is faster."

Buddy smiled at Will. "Well, why don't you go take a ride?"

He tried to walk around Will. But Will moved quickly to block his path. "No. Really, man. My car is faster than yours."

Buddy's smile faded. "What do you want? Want me to buy you a trophy?"

Sara stepped up behind Will. She put a hand on the shoulder of Will's leather jacket, her eyes on Buddy. "He doesn't want to race you, Will," she said softly.

"You got *that* right," Buddy sneered.

"Afraid to race the Cataluna?" Will challenged.

Buddy tried once again to get past Will, but Will moved to block his escape. Buddy glanced up and caught a gleam of excitement in Sara's eyes.

She's enjoying this, he thought bitterly.

She's watching to see what I do. It's like she's *testing* me.

"You afraid to race that car?" Will repeated, narrowing his silvery eyes at Buddy.

"Give me a break," Buddy muttered. "I'm outta here."

Will refused to move. "I heard about your family," he said. "I heard you were all great drivers. Guess every family has to have one wimp."

Buddy felt a wave of anger swell up from his chest.

"Don't let him talk to you like that, Buddy!" Sara exclaimed.

"Okay, okay. I'll race you." The words escaped Buddy's mouth before he could even think about them.

"Tomorrow night. The Mill Road," Will said.

"I'll be there," Buddy replied.

part

2

chapter

6

I recognized William at once. Did he really think he could trick me by shortening his name to Will? He followed Buddy home to study the Cataluna—to study me. To decide if the Doom Car and I were one and the same.

Did William really think he could fool me? So pale, so troubled. Not at all like Buddy's other friends.

Not at all like Buddy and his brothers.

None of the people I had encountered in my strange journey through the twentieth century called to me as strongly as did this new boy.

Foolish Will Parker.

He probably is not certain that my spirit inhabits the Cataluna. I once tricked William into murdering an innocent girl. He thought my spirit inhabited *her*. How can he be certain of anything after that?

But he suspects—because of all the deaths I have caused.

I don't suspect. I know. And I cannot wait to rid the earth of you, William . . . Will . . . Parker.

"She's good looking," Will admitted. "I'll give her that much."

Buddy stood in front of the Cataluna as Will slowly circled the car. Sara watched them both eagerly.

This is Sara's dream come true, Buddy thought, disgusted. Two guys competing for her.

So what do you want her for? I bet that's what Stan would ask me.

I want her because she's my girlfriend. *Mine*. Who is this Will guy to show up at my friend's party? Come on to my girlfriend? And try to make me look dumb.

"She might even be fast," Will reluctantly added. "But that doesn't mean you can drive her. And it doesn't mean you could beat me."

"Buddy is a great driver," Sara told Will. Then she smiled at the pale, blond boy. "But I hear you might be even better."

I get it, Buddy thought. If I win the race, I win Sara. If I lose, I lose Sara.

Warnings flashed through Buddy's mind. This car killed Stan. It's cursed. It kills everyone who gets in it.

Drive this car and you'll hurt Dad in a way nothing else could.

Buddy turned to Will. "You know, you sure talk a lot. What are you trying to prove?"

"Nothing." Will smirked at Buddy. "You're the only one here with something to prove." He winked at Sara.

Buddy burned. He understood what Will meant. One glance at Sara told him everything he needed to know. If Buddy didn't race, he and Sara were through.

No way, he told himself. No way. Sara is *my* girl. I lost Stan. I'm not losing her.

He glared at Will. "See you tomorrow night."

He saw a pleased grin spread over Sara's pretty face.

The next night Buddy lay on top of his bed—waiting. He would show Will. And Sara, too. And anybody else who thought he was afraid—afraid of racing, or of racing Will, or of racing the Cataluna.

He was sick of people talking behind his back. Talking about Stan. And Sara. And now the race.

What happened to my life? he wondered. Everything is upside down.

Well, not for long, he told himself. Everything gets fixed tonight. After tonight people are going to be talking only about how I won the race.

He glanced at the clock. 11:06. He heard his dad snoring. He thought about leaving early.

No. Stick to the plan. Wait until eleven-thirty. Wait until you're sure Dad won't wake up. You'll still get home way before Sean. Don't blow it before you're even out of the house.

Buddy took a deep breath. He remembered some advice Stan gave him once. "You have to clear the butterflies before a race. Bad nerves will kill you."

Bad nerves or a bad car, Buddy thought.

He couldn't take lying still for another second. Buddy rolled off his bed and crossed the room to his desk. He glanced at the clock again. Not even a full minute had passed.

He spotted his hand-held *Blazing Racers* game. A few rounds and it will be time to go, he thought. The game had cool graphics, fast cars, and every time you crashed, a blazing winged skull flapped up out of the car, laughing as it flew off into the clouds.

The first round got him through seven minutes. The next round—four more minutes. Another round—two more minutes. Another round—two more minutes. Another round—one more minute.

And then every round ended in seconds. Buddy couldn't keep the small electronic cars on the road. Each one crashed almost immediately, sending another blazing skull winging its way to heaven. Laughing as it went.

Buddy tossed the game onto his bed.

What am I going to do? Buddy stared at the game lying facedown on his bed. I can't even drive a toy car. What's the matter with me?

He checked the clock again. 11:29. Good enough.

He grabbed his silver-and-black Chevy baseball

cap, jammed it on, and then crept to the bedroom door. He cracked it open and listened. All quiet, except for his dad's snoring down the hall.

Buddy swung the door wide and stepped as far out into the hall as he could. He needed to clear the squeaky board outside his room. It always woke his dad.

Got to be silent, he reminded himself with each step. Got to get out of here.

Buddy reached the stairs without making a sound. He moved down them, careful to stay close to the wall. Pressure on the ends of the steps didn't make half the noise stepping on the worn middles did.

Holding his breath, he reached the kitchen without waking his father. He stopped at the refrigerator, grabbed a carton of milk, took a long slug and replaced the carton. Then he slipped out the back door.

In less than a minute he stood outside the garage. He swung open the big door slowly, holding it tightly to keep it from making any noise. He made every motion slowly, thinking through every step before he performed it.

I have to pull this off. Everything is riding on it.

He stepped through the open doorway. The white Cataluna gleamed, even in the dim light.

"We'll show them," he muttered. "We'll bring *doom* to anyone who tries to take what is ours."

A flash of light from one of the neighboring houses played across the front of the Cataluna.

Buddy slid in behind the wheel. The smell of the red leather seats filled his nose. His lungs.

Stan would want me to do this—to race this guy, Buddy told himself. He wouldn't want me to be a wimp.

Buddy started up the car as gently as he could. He fed it only enough gas to keep the motor running. He wanted to mash the pedal to the floor, wanted to hear the Cataluna's powerful engine roar through the garage. But he knew better.

He'd have plenty of time for making noise after the race. After he showed everyone what a phony Will was. After he had Sara back. After everyone knew that Buddy McCloy was everything his brother Stan had been.

Buddy backed the Cataluna down the driveway— slowly, carefully—motor low, lights out.

I can handle this car. No problem.

His eyes on his house—on his father's window—he allowed a smile to cross his face. No problem at all. Piece of cake.

Buddy heard a scream, then a sharp *crack!* The car bumped.

"Oh, no! I backed over someone!"

chapter

7

A shrill shriek.

"No! Oh, no!" Buddy shoved open the car door and leaped out.

"What happened?" Buddy shouted. "What happened?"

A boy, thirteen or fourteen years old, stood on the sidewalk, trembling, face twisted in horror.

"My skateboard!" he screamed. "You ran over my skateboard!"

Buddy let out a long sigh of relief. The kid wasn't hurt.

"I couldn't see you. It was too dark," Buddy stammered.

"You wrecked my skateboard. It went right under

55

your car and you wrecked it. And you're paying for it."

Buddy checked the house. Good, he thought. Dad's light is still off. He glanced at the Cataluna, gleaming even more brightly in the moonlight.

"No problem. I promise," he told the kid, glancing at his watch. "Come back tomorrow, Okay? I'll give you then money then."

The expression on the kid's face changed. He looked amazed—amazed at his good fortune. Then he turned and ran for home as if he didn't want to jinx it.

Buddy wiped his forehead. His hand shook. That was a close call. I'm more nervous than I thought, he realized. But it's too late to back down now.

Sliding into the driver's seat, he felt calmer. He could feel power vibrating through the Cataluna's wheel, the ivory ball of the stick shift, even through the seat and the floor.

He shut the door and continued out the driveway. If anyone is going to be backing down tonight, he told himself, it's not going to be me.

The front wheels of the Doom Car finished smashing the skateboard as Buddy backed into the street.

"You sure took your time getting here," Will called as Buddy climbed out of the Cataluna.

"I'm here now," Buddy replied softly. He checked out the small crowd around Will's car and found Sara.

Buddy stared at Will. He caught a trace of hesitation in the new kid's eyes.

He didn't think I would show, Buddy realized. He thought I was too afraid. Too afraid to go against my dad. Too afraid to drive the Doom Car.

A big smile broke across Buddy's face. He stared down "Racer's Lane," the town nickname for a mile and a half stretch of the Mill Road where all the jammers tested one another. The police seldom patrolled the area because the only thing along the stretch was the deserted old mill.

Buddy strolled over to Will's car. A Chevelle—a beauty with nice lines and a metal-flake cherry-red paint job. And no ordinary street model, either.

Even in the dark Buddy could tell that it had been tinkered with. The oversize scoop box on the hood let him know Will had installed a big block engine with some kind of high-rise manifold.

Will noticed Buddy studying his car. He leaned into the driver's window and popped the car's hood, showing off its engine. "Think you can beat that?"

Buddy glanced inside casually. What he saw rocked him. He hoped Will hadn't noticed his surprise.

Or Sara. She kept staring at them both, her eyes moving back and forth from Buddy to Will.

You ain't seen nothin' yet, Sara, Buddy thought. He made a show of yawning as he ran his eyes over Will's engine. Then he crossed his arms over his chest. "Yeah—so what do we have here? Weiand Hi-Ram, back vented for the street. Two Holley vacuum-secondary four barrels. You have all four of the side-hung bowls plumbed to the fuel log—which you didn't even need to do."

Buddy slammed down the hood and turned to Will. "Tells me you're too cautious. Sure you're up for racing in the dark? I wouldn't want you to get scared and mess up your little car."

"Very little chance of that, McCloy," snapped Will.

Buddy turned and walked away. "Then get in your car. Let's do it!"

Buddy slid behind the wheel of the Cataluna. He fastened his seat belt and shoulder harness. Shifting into gear, he pulled forward into the right-hand lane, forcing Will to cross behind him and take the left lane.

Joel Harper, a guy from Buddy's class, broke away from the crowd. He stripped off his jacket to use as a starting flag. "First one to the old mill wins," Joel called. He raised his watch.

Buddy revved the engine. He focused on the physical sensations as a way to stay calm. The sharp smell of gas in his nose. The roar of the engine. The car vibrating beneath him.

"Get ready . . ."

Joel moved his legs apart, and raised his jacket over his head.

"Set . . ."

Joel's arm twitched.

Here it comes, Buddy thought, his fingers poised above the stick shift. Itching.

"Go!" Joel whipped his jacket down.

The Cataluna's tires screeched as Buddy flew down the Mill Road. He glanced out the window. The Cataluna had only a few inches on Will's cherry-red Chevelle.

"Faster, baby," Buddy whispered, pleading with the car. "Faster." The Cataluna pulled a foot ahead.

Will's car responded with a burst of speed, moving a yard ahead of the Cataluna. Buddy could see Will laughing, his head tossed back, blond hair billowing behind him.

Grinding the gas pedal down, Buddy leaned over the steering wheel. He smiled as his front end pulled in line with the Chevelle's.

Buddy and Will held their positions. Buddy tried to force more speed out of the Cataluna. But the car had reached its limit.

Side by side.

Spin the wheel, Buddy suddenly thought. *A little nudge—and Will crashes and burns!*

Nothing hurts this car. There won't be a scratch.

"Do it," a voice inside his head urged.

Halfway to the mill. Buddy had only seconds to win.

"Do it. Do it."

Seconds to beat Will.

"Do it! Turn the wheel. Give Will a little bump. Make him crash."

Seconds to get Sara back.

"Do it!" the voice urged.

No, Buddy thought. No! I don't want to kill him!

"Do it! Now!"

Buddy turned the wheel.

He heard a piercing wail.

A wail of pain?

No.

Flashing red-and-blue lights in the mirror.

The police.

chapter
8

*B*uddy downshifted and pulled to the side of the road. How fast had he been going? A hundred? A hundred and ten?

Oh, wow. A ticket, Buddy thought. Maybe two. Maybe even an appearance.

Buddy's stomach tightened. They'll call Dad. He'll find out I drove the Cataluna.

The squad car rolled up beside him. One of the officers beamed his flashlight into Buddy's face. "Well, well. One of the racing McCloy brothers."

Buddy squinted into the light. Officer Beard coldly stared back at him. Buddy had been stopped by the man before. "Haven't you learned your lesson yet?"

"Knock it off, Beard," the other officer snapped.

Her voice sounded familiar. Buddy leaned forward so he could see the driver—an older woman with short dark hair. Officer Barnett. Perfect, Buddy thought. I had to get stopped by a friend of Dad's.

"What's the hurry?" Beard asked calmly. "Who were you racing?"

Buddy stared out through the windshield. The road stretched empty and dark. He quickly checked both sides of the Cataluna and glanced in the rearview mirror.

Where is Will? Buddy wondered. He was right next to me! Where did he go?

Three days later Buddy sat in the living room staring absently at the television. He held the remote in his hand, but he didn't use it.

Buddy didn't care what show came on. All he could see was his race with Will. He replayed it again and again in his mind.

He realized he'd been lucky—really lucky. The police showed up seconds before he tried to run Will off the road.

But the police didn't know that. They hadn't seen Will's car, probably because the white Cataluna was so much brighter.

And they didn't even give me a ticket, Buddy thought. Or call Dad. They felt too bad about what happened to Stan.

"You're still looking out for me, aren't you, Stan?"

Buddy whispered. But I can't do anything right without you here. Not anything.

Buddy closed his eyes and saw himself jerking the steering wheel. Aiming at Will.

I would have killed him, Buddy thought. He would be dead now. And I would be a murderer.

Buddy shuddered. Was getting Sara back *that* important?

What happened to me? Why did I lose it like that?

Buddy had been avoiding everyone—including Sara. He went to school, then hurried straight home. Then he did his homework and watched TV. Or slept. He slept a lot.

But he wished Sara would call him. Every time the phone rang he found himself hoping it was Sara.

She doesn't care about you, he thought angrily. When are you going to figure that out?

The doorbell rang. Buddy jumped up from the couch. Who is it?

Sara! Sara used to drop by all the time.

Buddy brushed back his hair with his fingers and rushed to answer the door. Don't blow it, he warned himself. Be friendly, but don't fall all over her.

He grabbed the doorknob and yanked the door open.

"Hi, stranger." Marisol smiled at him.

Buddy tried to hide his disappointment.

"I haven't run into you in days," Marisol said.

"I—I've been keeping to myself, I guess."

"Well, that's no good. Want to get a Coke or something?"

"With you?" Buddy asked. Stupid question, he thought. I'm acting like the biggest geek in the universe again.

"Who else?" she teased. "Why do you think I came over?"

Buddy laughed. "I'll be right back," he told Marisol. He ducked into his room and grabbed his keys. Then he ran out the front door and pulled Marisol to the driveway.

I needed to get out, Buddy realized. He suddenly wanted to be around people again. "Want to drive to the mall?" he asked.

"Great," she answered.

They climbed into Buddy's old Chevy. Buddy pulled out of the driveway and headed toward Division Street. He felt relieved that Marisol hadn't asked him to take the Cataluna. He didn't want anything to do with the Doom Car. Not after what he almost did to Will.

Buddy cranked up the radio and rolled down his window. Yeah, he thought, it feels great to get out of the house.

A few minutes later he pulled into the mall parking lot and slipped into a spot. "Where to?" he asked Marisol as they climbed out of the car.

"You pick," she answered. "I'm new in town, remember?"

Buddy led Marisol to the Doughnut Hole. He

ordered two large Cokes. "Want a doughnut, too?" he asked.

"Definitely," Marisol told him. Buddy watched her as she carefully studied the doughnuts in the glass case.

"This isn't part of the SAT test," Buddy joked. "They aren't going to ask you what color sprinkles are on the average doughnut."

"I know, I know," Marisol replied. "I've almost decided."

"Give us a large box of doughnut holes—assorted," Buddy told the clerk. He turned and smiled at Marisol. "Now you can have one of each."

"You're a genius," Marisol teased. They took their doughnuts and sodas back out into the mall and found a bench.

Buddy laughed as Marisol taste-tested each type of doughnut for him. He felt more relaxed than he had in days.

"Let's walk around," Buddy suggested when they finished their food. "I feel a massive sugar rush coming on."

Buddy and Marisol wandered in and out of the stores, talking. Buddy told her about some of the things he and Stan used to do together. It felt good to talk about his brother. Marisol didn't act uncomfortable the way most people did when Stan's name came up.

Buddy started feeling hungry for some real food, so they headed toward Pete's Pizza. Are you really hungry? A little voice in Buddy's head asked him. Or do you just want kids from school to see you with Marisol?

Both, Buddy decided. What's wrong with that? I want some pizza. And I want to make sure everyone knows I'm not broken up over Sara. I want to prove that I don't need her at all.

Buddy stopped outside the restaurant and stared into the big front window. A few feet away he spotted the only two people in the world he didn't want to see. Sara and Will.

They were sharing a pizza—pepperoni and mushrooms. That's what Buddy and Sara always ordered.

I should be the one sitting there, Buddy thought. I should be sharing that pizza with Sara. Not Will.

He forgot all about Marisol as he stared through the window. He watched Sara laugh at something Will said.

Why is she interested in that creep? I raced him. I was winning. He ran away. What is she doing with him? What is so *great* about him?

Buddy watched Sara lift a piece of pepperoni from the pizza. The melted cheese stuck to it. The cheese stretched out almost a foot before it snapped.

Sara grabbed the end of the cheese and shoved it into her mouth. Then she popped the pepperoni into Will's. The string of cheese linked them together.

Sara had done the same thing to Buddy about a hundred times.

"Nooooooooooooo!!" Buddy howled without realizing it.

Pain shot through his hand and up his arm.

He heard Marisol cry out. Faces turned to stare at him.

"Your hand!" Marisol cried. "Your hand!"

Buddy slowly raised his hand in front of his eyes.

He gaped at it. Mangled. Broken. Blood-soaked. "What have I done?" he asked himself. "What have I done?"

chapter

9

$H$is mouth open in shock, Buddy turned his gaze from his hand to the restaurant window. To his horror, the window was smashed. Shards of jagged glass littered the floor.

I shoved my hand through the window, Buddy realized.

Without thinking, without even realizing.

Buddy heard Marisol asking him if he was okay. He couldn't answer.

Through the shattered window, he stared at Sara. Did you see that, Sara? Did you see what you made me do?

He raised his blood-covered hand as if showing it

off to her. Do you think Will cares about you this much?

On the other side of the glass Sara returned his stare, her face twisted in surprise, in confusion.

Marisol gently grabbed his hand. She dabbed at the blood with a wad of tissues. "It's a deep cut," she said softly. "You're going to need stitches."

But it wasn't as bad as Buddy had thought. No broken bones. He could move his fingers. Just a deep cut along the knuckles.

"Buddy, let's go—" Marisol urged. "We've got to get you to the emergency room."

But he pulled his hand away. And with an angry cry he burst through the door, into the crowded restaurant, up to Sara's booth.

Faces turned. Someone uttered a cry of surprise.

"Buddy—" Sara jumped to her feet. "What do you think you're doing?"

He glared at her, holding his injured hand in front of him. "What do you think *you're* doing?" His voice came out high and shrill. His heart pounded. The lights suddenly seemed too bright.

"Whoa, take it easy, man," Will said, raising both hands to signal halt.

"You—you broke the window!" Sara cried, staring at Buddy's hand. "Are you *crazy?*"

"You'd better get that looked at," Will said. "It looks really bad. If you have glass stuck inside—"

"Never mind that!" Buddy cried, gripping the table edge. "What are you doing here with Sara?"

A thin smile played over Will's lips. "Having pizza."

"Buddy, you don't have a right—" Sara started, still standing, arms crossed over her chest. "You really—"

Buddy gripped the table harder. Why was the room suddenly tilting? Why were the lights so bright?

Ignoring the aching pain that throbbed through his hand, he narrowed his eyes at Will. "What happened to you the other night? Where'd you go?"

"I cut off down a side road. I didn't want to be hassled by the cops." He lowered his eyes to Buddy's hand. "Really, man. You'd better get to a doctor. You need stitches on that."

Buddy stared furiously at Sara. But his words were for Will. "We haven't finished. We haven't finished our race. Friday night. Meet me at the bottom of River Road. We'll finish it then."

Why did he sound so breathless? Why was the room tilting and spinning?

He struggled to hear Will's reply. Something about the Cataluna.

"Yeah. Right. I'll be in the Cataluna," Buddy promised. He spun away, casting one last glance at Sara. "Don't chicken out. We'll finish it this time."

He didn't hear Will's reply. He saw two waitresses hurrying toward him. He saw another one on the phone, probably calling the security guards about the window he broke.

Holding his injured hand, Buddy turned and ran.

Buddy tried to find Marisol at school the next day. But he wasn't sure she even went to Shadyside High. He'd never seen her there. Maybe she went to a private school.

She hadn't waited for him after he burst into the pizza restaurant. Who could blame her? Buddy thought glumly as he wandered through the halls. I acted like a jerk. She'll probably never talk to me again, and I deserve it.

He felt a wave of regret wash over him. Marisol was terrific. Prettier than most of the girls at his school. She listened when he talked. She went out of her way to be with him.

Well, he thought, I don't have to worry about seeing her again. She comes and gets me out of the house, makes me feel better than I have in weeks. And what do I do? I smash up a restaurant window because I'm jealous about my old girlfriend.

Smart guy, McCloy. Real smart guy.

Buddy turned toward the exit. School was over, but what did it matter? He had nowhere to go. Nothing to do.

He didn't feel like hanging out with his friends. And he didn't have a girlfriend anymore. Not even a possible girlfriend.

Why did I do such a bonehead thing? he asked himself again and again. How did I get so out of control, so crazy I didn't even know what I was doing?

I've always been a little hotheaded, he admitted to himself. But I've never done anything like that before.

It's Sara's fault, he decided.

When I saw her with Will, I just snapped.

Buddy shoved open the front door to the school and shuffled across the grass to the parking lot.

He moved slowly. What difference did it make whether he hurried or not? What difference did anything make anymore?

Maybe I shouldn't even go to River Road on Friday, Buddy thought. I mean, what would be the point? Going through the hassle of sneaking out the Cataluna again—for what? Somebody tell me . . . for what?

To his surprise, he saw Sara waiting for him, leaning against his car. He didn't speed up his pace. He kept ambling slowly until he stood beside her. "What's up?"

"Just wanted to make sure you're okay," she said, avoiding his eyes. She shifted her backpack on her shoulders.

"Yeah. I'm okay. I'm great. Just great," he replied sarcastically.

She stared at the bandage on his hand. "I can't believe you did that."

He let out a bitter laugh. "I can't believe it, either."

A long silence. Sara pushed back her hair. "You're angry with me, huh?"

The words burst out of Buddy before he could stop them. "Why are you hanging out with that creep Will? I thought you and I were going together."

She reacted sharply. "Give me a break, Buddy. I saw you with that other girl."

"Huh? You mean Marisol?"

"If you can go out with another girl, why don't I have the right to see Will?"

"But, Sara—I—I—"

She pushed away from the car and started across the parking lot. "Glad your hand is okay. See you Friday night. At the race."

"Sara—" He called after her, but he didn't know what to say.

Was she jealous of Marisol? Or was she just using Marisol as an excuse for her hanging out with Will?

Would winning the race Friday night impress Sara? Would it impress her enough to dump Will and come back to him?

It's all too confusing, Buddy thought, watching her jog across the parking lot.

Too confusing.

He only knew one thing for sure.

He had to win that race Friday night. He'd do *anything* to win that race.

chapter

10

Buddy snapped off the tiny reading light on his nightstand. Same drill as the last time, he told himself. Get out of the house without waking Dad. Get the Cataluna and beat Will for good.

He reached the garage door with no problems, then stared back at the house. It stood dark and quiet. No one knew what he was up to.

Good, Buddy thought. Let's keep it that way.

Buddy eased open the garage door. His eyes roamed over the gleaming white body of the Cataluna. He loved to stare at it.

It's the most beautiful car I've ever seen. The most beautiful car in the world.

Everything about it is perfect.

But as he stared at the shining car, a pair of small, dark shadows edged out of the Cataluna's open windows.

The shadows floated slowly. So slowly Buddy thought they were a trick of the light. As they hovered over the car, they grew larger, moved faster.

More shadows billowed up out of the car. Two at a time, they twisted through the windows, floated into the pale garage light.

What are those things? What are they? Buddy wondered, suddenly cold with fear.

Run! Run now! he urged himself.

But it was too late. He couldn't move. He couldn't move at all.

And the shadows slid closer.

Some of the dark patches swirled into the air, floated around Buddy's head. They felt cold. They froze his skin without even touching it.

And they smelled so bad. Buddy held his breath, trying to shut out the foul, putrid smell.

Buddy tasted something sour in the back of his throat. The rank odor clung to his clothes, his face— filling his nose, burning his eyes.

He tried to scream, tried to run . . . but he couldn't.

Terror swept over him. But he knew it wasn't the fear that held him in place. No, not the fear.

Something else. Something outside of him. Something stronger.

The shadows began to twist into solid forms.

Buddy gaped in horror as they took on colors and shapes.

Decaying faces floated above Buddy, skin hanging like rags, eyes swinging by nerve endings, worms crawling through toothless jaws.

Buddy couldn't turn away. He couldn't close his eyes. He had to watch.

More ugly faces floated from the Cataluna. They began to circle Buddy's head. One face slashed Buddy's cheek with broken, rotted teeth. One kissed him with moldy green lips.

Then all the shadow faces began to pull together.

No, Buddy thought. Please, no. Please, please, please, no!

As he stared helplessly the heads folded into each other. The gruesome faces blended into one hideous face. The giant face hovered for a moment—then flew straight at Buddy.

Its mouth opened impossibly wide. The torn lips twisted into a scream.

But no sound came out. No sound. Something worse.

Insects poured from the mouth. Spiders and flies and hundreds of white maggots spilled over the garage floor.

"No—no—no—no—noooooooo!" The scream broke from Buddy's lips. He screamed again. Screamed until his throat ached.

And then Buddy recognized the horrible face attacking him.

It was his own face.

The force that held Buddy suddenly released him. He scrambled into a corner.

Corner? What corner? Where?

Buddy's eyes darted frantically from side to side. Where am I? Where is my face?

I'm in my room, he realized. I'm not in the garage, I'm in my room.

I'm inside. Safe. The car is outside and I'm inside. Inside. Safe.

Buddy wiped his forehead with his pillow. Only a dream, he realized.

But what did it mean?

Was it warning me not to race again? Or was it warning me not to back out of the race? What did those faces mean? What? What!

Stan, Buddy thought suddenly. Maybe Stan sent me the dream. Maybe he's still trying to look out fer me. Trying to help me from the grave.

That's crazy, Buddy thought. I've got to calm down. Got to stop acting so crazy.

"Who cares about a dumb nightmare?" he mumbled. He got up and headed to the kitchen.

Something to eat—that would make him feel better. A sandwich and some milk. That would fix him up.

"No matter what it means. No matter what—I'm racing the Cataluna on Friday. Then I'm getting Sara back."

* * *

Buddy sat at the kitchen table the next morning staring at his breakfast—a cherry Pop-Tart and a glass of milk.

"Breakfast of champions, huh?" his father asked on his way out the door "You can't make it through your morning classes on that."

A few minutes later Sean entered the kitchen, stretching and yawning. He poured himself a glass of juice. "That's all you're having?" he asked Buddy.

Buddy shrugged. "I had a late snack last night. I'm not too hungry now."

"Oh," Sean answered. "I thought you had a guilty conscience."

"And what's that crack supposed to mean?" Buddy snapped.

"I thought maybe you started feeling bad about going against Dad's orders."

Buddy felt all his muscles tighten. He glared at his brother. "What are you talking about?"

"Hey, don't play innocent with me." Sean pulled a skillet out of the cupboard. "I ran into Officer Barnett yesterday. I heard all about you tearing up the Mill Road—in the Cataluna."

"I didn't hurt anything," Buddy answered defensively.

"That's not the point, is it, Gilhooley?" Sean asked, still holding the skillet. "Dad told us not to touch that jinxed car. If you mess it up, we wouldn't get back any of the cash we sank into it. That wouldn't help much, would it?"

"Don't call me Gilhooley. Only Stan could call me that." Buddy took a bite of the Pop-Tart, hoping Sean would drop the subject of the Cataluna. He didn't.

"Did you stop to think what it would do to Dad if you got yourself hurt in that thing? It killed Stan. Dad's still tearing himself up over that. We all are. If you even got a little scratch or something driving it, it would make Dad go psycho."

"Yeah, yeah . . . whatever." Buddy started breaking the Pop-Tart into little pieces.

"Hey—be as big a creep as you want," Sean told him, setting the skillet on the stove. "But stay away from the Cataluna."

"Don't worry," Buddy replied angrily. He hated the way Sean had started acting when Stan died—as if he was in charge of the world or something. "I only need it once more. Then I don't care if Dad has it box-pressed for scrap."

"Once more?" Sean turned around and stared at Buddy. "I don't get you. What could be so important that you'd even think of taking it out again?"

"I have to. I need to race it one more time to get Sara away from this guy Will."

"You're crazy." Sean pulled three eggs out of the refrigerator. "Forget her. She's not worth it. What about that new girl—Marisol? She seems really nice."

"Marisol's nice," Buddy admitted. "But she isn't Sara."

"Well, too bad." Sean headed for the stove. "Because you aren't racing that thing again. I won't let you. I'll tell Dad if I have to."

Buddy leaped out of his chair and grabbed Sean from behind. "You're not doing anything!"

Buddy spun his brother around violently. Sean stumbled, trying to keep his balance. The three eggs went flying, two breaking against the refrigerator, one on the floor.

"You won't stop me!" Buddy screamed, grabbing his brother by the shirt.

Sean stood absolutely still.

He's scared, Buddy realized. Sean's scared of me.

"I mean it, Sean—you're not stopping me," Buddy repeated. "Nobody's stopping me! I'm taking the Cataluna tomorrow night!"

"All right, all right." Sean pushed Buddy away and strode to the other side of the kitchen. "Fine. Go ahead. Do what you want."

"Stay out of my way, Sean," Buddy warned. He grabbed his backpack and headed for the door.

He stopped and snatched up a dish towel, then threw it at his brother. "And don't forget to clean up your mess."

Buddy could feel Sean's eyes on his back as he closed the door. I don't care what Sean thinks, he told himself. I don't care.

Buddy didn't care about anything. Except teaching Will the lesson he deserved. Except getting Sara back.

Except racing the Cataluna.

* * *

THE DEADLY FIRE

Buddy slammed the door and tossed his backpack onto the kitchen table. Friday afternoon, he thought. Finally. The past two days of school felt like twenty years.

Be smart, he told himself. Don't let Dad see you all nervous and bouncing around and obviously waiting for something. Do your homework.

Buddy unzipped the backpack and dumped his books onto the table. You've got enough to keep you busy all night. So do it. Keep busy.

He stuck to his plan, knocking off one assignment after another. Hour after hour.

Down to one chapter of history to read. Perfect timing, he thought. Finish this and you're off. No problem.

Smiling, Buddy opened his book and turned to the chapter on the *Hindenburg*—a dirigible that crashed in New Jersey in 1937. Buddy highlighted the fact that the *Hindenburg* wouldn't have crashed if it had been filled with the right kind of gas.

Quiz question definitely. Remember that—gas.

Gas?

The word sounded in Buddy's head. Seeing it highlighted tugged at his brain.

Gas! The Cataluna! Gas!

Buddy slammed his book. I planned to fill it after the race the other night. Then I got pulled over, and I forgot all about it.

Now I don't know if I have enough gas for tonight.

What if I run out of gas halfway to River Road? What if I run out of gas during the race?

I have to leave now, he thought. Sean is upstairs. Dad came home and went out again.

Buddy sprang to his feet, almost knocking his chair over backward. He ran through the kitchen and burst out the back door. He hurried to the garage and threw open the door.

"Huh?"

He uttered a low cry when he saw that the Cataluna was *gone!*

chapter

11

*B*uddy stared into the empty garage.

His heart pounded. He blinked several times, trying to blink the car back into view. Where is it? Did Dad sell it?

No, Buddy reasoned, struggling to calm himself. He would have told us. If he got rid of the Cataluna, he would have been so happy. He would have told us.

So did Dad take it out when he left earlier?

No. He would never drive it anywhere. He hates the car. Besides, I would have known. I would have heard it. Dad definitely didn't take it.

So that meant Sean did.

Buddy turned slowly back toward the house. Of course. Sean. Who else?

Buddy shut the garage door slowly, deliberately. He made his way back to the house in the same purposeful, steady manner.

His anger built with every step.

By the time he started up the stairs to Sean's room, he felt calm. A seething calm. A white-hot calm.

Who do you think you are, Sean? he thought. I told you to stay out of this. But no, you wouldn't listen. Oh, no, you never listen.

Buddy's hand closed on the knob of Sean's door.

Well, listen to this, big brother.

He threw Sean's door open with a crash.

Sean lay on his bed reading a manual about Camaro restoration. Buddy grabbed him and jerked him up off the bed before he could look up from the book.

"Where did you hide it? Where?"

Sean stared at his brother blankly.

Buddy knocked the manual out of his hand. "Where? Where? Where?"

"What's your problem? What are you talking about?" Sean demanded.

Buddy dragged Sean to the floor and jumped on top of him. "I'll make you talk!" he screamed.

Sean grabbed Buddy, and they rolled across the floor. Sean ended up on top.

Buddy let out a furious groan and flipped Sean over him. Then he rolled on top of Sean and drove his knee into the carpet so they couldn't roll again.

He grabbed Sean's head in his hands. "What did you do with the Cataluna?"

"I'm not going to tell you. There's no way I'm going to let you race that car! You're crazy, Buddy! I can't let you!" Sean cried.

"Tell me! Tell me where it is!"

In a fury Buddy banged his brother's head against the carpet. Sean groaned from the pain of the impact. Buddy let go of Sean's head and punched his brother in the face—once, twice.

Blood spilled from Sean's mouth. Buddy didn't care. "Tell me where the Cataluna is! Tell me!"

Sean struggled underneath Buddy, clawing at his brother. Buddy slapped his hands away, punching Sean again—in the chest, in the face. Now Buddy's hands were smeared with blood.

"Tell me!" Buddy screamed. He grabbed Sean's head in his hands again and slammed it against the carpet.

"Tell me where it is!"

Sean didn't answer.

Buddy slammed Sean's head against the carpet again.

"Tell me!"

No reply.

Buddy bounced his brother's head off the carpet again. Again.

Until Sean's eyes rolled up into his head. And his body went limp beneath Buddy.

Buddy stared down into Sean's white eyes.

His mind suddenly cleared. Buddy gasped in horror.

"What did I do?"

Buddy gazed down at his bloody hands. He uttered a long, high wail of pain.

"I've killed him. I've killed my own brother!"

chapter

___

12

*B*uddy pressed his ear to Sean's chest.

"Oh, no—oh, please—oh, please don't be dead, Sean. Oh, please, don't be dead!"

Leaning over Sean, Buddy listened hard. His own heart hammered so loudly, he still couldn't tell if Sean had a heartbeat.

Buddy straightened up. He took a deep breath and held it, forcing himself to calm down.

Then he bent over his brother's chest again.

"He's alive!" Buddy backed away, uttering a sigh of relief.

Sean's alive! he thought. He's going to be okay!

Buddy stared at the blood on his hands. "Sean," he

said softly, "I'm sorry. I'm really sorry. Are you all right?"

Sean groaned. He rubbed the back of his head. Then he began to cough.

"Are you all right?" Buddy demanded again.

"What do you care?" Sean mumbled. "You want to start over again? Make sure you did a good job?"

"Sean . . ."

Buddy didn't know what else to say. He had gone nuts. He had totally lost it. How could he have done that to Sean? How could he have tried to kill his own brother?

Will and Sara and the Cataluna were all making him crazy. He didn't know what to do anymore.

"Sean, I—" Buddy began again. "I messed up."

"Forget it. I don't want to hear it."

"I wanted to say I'm sorry."

Sean stared up at him silently, wiping the blood off his mouth.

Buddy's eyes stung with tears. "I mean it. I totally lost it."

Sean groaned and struggled to get up off the floor. Buddy helped him over to the bed, glad that Sean didn't try to push him away.

"It's just that I need the Cataluna so badly," Buddy tried to explain.

"Yeah, right," Sean muttered bitterly.

"Listen, I'm really sorry."

"Yeah. Sure." Sean dug around in his pocket. He pulled something out and tossed it to Buddy.

The key ring for the Cataluna.

Buddy stared at the keys glistening in his hand.

"Go on, take it. Go on," Sean urged.

"Sean . . ." Buddy wanted to tell his brother that the race didn't matter—that nothing mattered except Sean.

"I put the car over at my friend Jeff's house. Figured I'd move it back tonight after it was too late for you to make your race."

Sean worked his jaw back and forth, making sure all his teeth were still in place. "Figured you'd be upset. Didn't expect you to try and kill me."

"I'm sorry," Buddy said again, forcing himself to meet his brother's gaze.

"Not as sorry as you're going to be if you drive that car," Sean said quietly.

Buddy hesitated, not understanding what Sean meant. "What?" he finally asked. "You going to tell Dad?"

Sean stared at his brother for a long moment. Then he shook his head. "No. Why should I get him all upset and worried? I don't care what you do anymore. I mean it."

Buddy couldn't speak.

"You go and run your race and get your little girlfriend back. You're not worth worrying about," Sean declared.

Hurt and confused, Buddy backed away from his brother.

"But I'm warning you, Buddy," Sean said, his voice

low and serious. "This is a mistake. A terrible mistake."

"Sean, please—"

"Listen to me, little brother. What you did to me is nothing compared to what you're about to do to yourself."

Buddy arrived at Jeff's house a few minutes later. The image of Sean's bloody face stayed with him the entire way, frozen in Buddy's mind. And Sean's words echoed: *This is a mistake. A terrible mistake.*

I wanted to kill my own brother. Buddy couldn't lie to himself. I truly wanted to kill Sean. And I almost did.

But it's over, Buddy promised himself. Over.

He had to get the Cataluna back in the garage before his father came home. After that, he would never touch the car again.

As Buddy hurried up Jeff's driveway, the image of Sean's bloody face began to melt. Began to twist and change, mutating into one of the hideous faces from his nightmare.

"Forget it," Buddy muttered. "You don't need to scare me anymore. I've learned my lesson."

But the face didn't go away. It split into two. Two rotting faces spinning through his brain.

The faces divided again and again.

By the time he reached the Cataluna, every face from his nightmare had returned. Including the last face. The most frightening one of all.

His own.

His face began to laugh. All the hundreds of faces laughed. Were they all laughing at him?

Buddy the fool. Buddy the coward. Buddy the killer.

"Shut up! Shut up!" Buddy cried.

Buddy quits and runs away. And Will gets Sara. Will wins everything. Will wins Sara.

"Stop. Leave me alone!" Buddy yelled.

Will gets to touch her . . . to kiss her.

Buddy squeezed his eyes shut. The voices in his head grew louder. The terrible faces grew brighter.

I'm going crazy, Buddy thought. Crazy. I can't take it. I can't.

"All right!" he cried, his voice trembling. "All right, I'll go. I'll go! I'll go to the race! But please, please, please leave me alone."

The voices stopped. The faces from his nightmare faded away.

"Leave me alone."

It took all of Buddy's concentration to slide the ignition key into its slot. He turned it, fed the gas, released the clutch as he found the right gear. He pulled out of the driveway.

His home lay to the right.

Buddy turned left.

Left. Toward Park Drive. The fastest way to River Road.

part
___
3

chapter

13

William—you are so close now. I know I am about to win my final triumph. I know.

I am going to crush you, Will. I am going to destroy you. You will never hunt Cataluna down again.

Are you wondering if I am ready for this race? For our last battle?

William Parker—you cannot imagine how ready I am.

First I will let you know that you have found me. Then I will drive you to your doom.

Buddy's fingers slid on the slick white enamel of the Cataluna's steering wheel. Sweat dripped down his back, gluing his shirt to his skin.

I almost killed Sean, he thought. I almost killed my own brother. Over a stupid race. Over a girl who treats me like dirt.

Over a car that killed Stan.

"Forget about it, Buddy. Forget about Sean and Stan. Let's have some fun."

The radio has been disconnected for months, Buddy thought. I'm hearing things again. Not a good sign.

The race. Got to focus on the race. Got to focus on beating Will.

Will is dead meat. I'm going to kill him. Kill him!

"Yes, kill him!" a girl's voice replied.

Soft, teasing laughter filled the car.

I didn't hear anything, Buddy told himself. I didn't.

He forced himself to remember everything he knew about River Road. It's the most dangerous place to race around here, he remembered. A lot of people won't drive on River Road at all when it's wet.

Of course, most people don't drive like Buddy McCloy, he told himself. He began to feel more confident as he sped along.

And most people don't have a car like the Cataluna.

Yes! Will is history! Buddy pressed down on the accelerator.

All I have to do is beat him to the dogleg. Once we hit that curve heading to the bridge, it's all over.

There is barely enough room for *one* car on that stretch.

And that one car will be the Cataluna, Buddy thought. Will will be lucky if his car doesn't end up in the Cononoka River—with the other cars already down there. Cars of other drivers who thought they could master the dogleg.

But I'm better than those guys, too, Buddy told himself. I'm better than all of them!

Up ahead, Buddy spotted Will's cherry-red Chevelle and a bunch of kids from school. No one wants to miss this race, Buddy told himself.

He pulled up beside the Chevelle and immediately searched the crowd for Sara. He found her standing next to Will, with her arm around his waist.

Figures, Buddy thought glumly.

He climbed out of the Cataluna and slammed the door. To his surprise, Marisol came running over, her long brown hair flying across her eyes.

"Marisol, I'm sorry about the other day. I—"

"That doesn't matter," Marisol interrupted. "Buddy, I came to try and stop you. Please don't race this car." She grabbed his hand and pulled him away from the Cataluna.

"Whoa. Relax. I've been in a lot of races," Buddy boasted.

"Someone's going to get hurt. Maybe killed," Marisol insisted.

Buddy stared at Marisol. Her chin trembled. She seemed really frightened.

She cares about me, he realized.

"I promise I'll be careful," he told Marisol.

"Please!" she cried, holding on to him. "Please don't race tonight. Forget about it. Go home before something horrible happens."

"Chickening out?" someone yelled. Buddy recognized the voice. Sara.

He slowly turned around. Sara stood on the roof of Will's car, her hands on her hips. She wore tight jeans with holes in the knees and Will's black knee-length jacket.

"Come on, chicken! Are you going to race or not?" she yelled.

"Go, Sara!" Mollie shouted from the middle of the crowd.

Buddy didn't bother to answer Sara. He turned to face Marisol. "You've been great," he told her. "You've been a real friend—and I've needed one lately. But please, you've got to understand—I have to do this. It's got to end tonight."

He turned and strode toward Will's car. His friends George and Peter broke out of the crowd and raced over to him.

"This is it—major payback night. Right, man?" George yelled, pounding Buddy on the back.

"Whatever you say, George." Buddy kept walking, not looking at his friends.

"You okay, Buddy? You up for this?" Peter asked quietly. "You don't have to race, you know."

"Never felt better," he replied. "Never been more up."

He stopped in front of Will and stared him in the eye. "Let's get this over with."

A strange smile played over Will's lips. "Not so fast, tough guy. I'm not sure which car I want to drive."

"Excuse me?" Buddy cried, confused.

"I don't need my car to beat you," Will bragged. "This isn't about who's got the baddest wheels. This is all about which one of us is the best driver."

"Ooooo!" a couple of guys in the crowd cat-called.

"What are you talking about?" Buddy demanded impatiently.

Everyone moved closer. The crowd grew quiet.

Sara jumped down from the Chevelle and moved between Buddy and Will. Her eyes darted back and forth between them.

She still thinks I'm doing this for her, Buddy thought. But I'm not. I'm doing it for me.

Will pulled a quarter out of his pocket. He held it up high, so everyone could see it.

"Okay—we'll flip to decide who drives which car," Will announced.

"Yeah, he knows he can't win in his hunk of junk!" George yelled from the crowd.

Buddy kept his eyes on Will.

"Heads I drive the Cataluna," Will said. "Tails you drive the Cataluna."

Buddy nodded. "Fine with me. Whatever."

He glanced around the crowd. Everyone was staring at the quarter in Will's fingers.

Tails, Buddy thought. Let it be tails. I want to drive the Cataluna one more time. Just one more time.

Will snapped his fingers, sending the quarter up into the air.

Up and up . . .

*T*he quarter fell back down.

Will caught it neatly in his left hand. He slapped the quarter down on the back of his right hand. Slowly he slid his fingers away.

"Heads!" Sara screamed.

"They're switching cars. Cool!" someone yelled.

Will shook his car keys in Buddy's face. "You up for it?"

Buddy scowled. But he plucked the keys out of Will's hand. "Man—you don't get it," Buddy told him. "You want to drive that thing, you go ahead."

Buddy suddenly wanted to tell Will about the nightmare. About all the dead faces.

He wanted to tell Will about the girl's voice he thought he heard in the Cataluna.

And he wanted to tell Will that if a great driver like Stan could get killed driving the white car, anyone could. Anyone.

But Will would think I was trying to pull some lame trick, Buddy thought. Trying to scare him out of driving the Doom Car. He wouldn't believe me. No one would.

Buddy fished in his jeans pocket and pulled out the keys to the Cataluna. He hesitated for just a moment. Then he flipped them to Will.

"Be my guest."

I got Buddy to go for the switch, Will thought. Perfect. Finally I have my shot at the Doom Car! I've waited so long.

He climbed behind the wheel of the Cataluna and checked out the unfamiliar console. Lights. Meters.

Will pushed himself deeper into the seat. He moved his hand back and forth between the steering wheel and stick shift, getting the feel of the car. He checked the distance between clutch and brake with his feet.

"You and me, Doom Car," he whispered, smiling. "Finally, it's you and me."

Will pulled out slowly onto River Road. He revved the engine, glancing over at Buddy. Buddy stared straight ahead.

Sara moved in front of the cars. She held up her hands. "Get ready!" she screamed.

She thrust out her hand, one finger extended.

"One!" the crowd shouted.

Sara pulled her hand back and thrust it out again, two fingers extended.

"Two!" came the cry.

Will stared at Sara intently. *Come on. Come on.*

Sara thrust out her hand again, three fingers extended.

"Three!"

Will slammed on the gas and rocketed away. He and Buddy stayed even as they sped toward the dogleg.

Faster, Will thought. Faster. Got to reach it first or the race is over.

The Chevelle inched in front of the Cataluna. Will pressed down on the accelerator. The Cataluna and the Chevelle sped side by side.

Out of the corner of his eye Will saw Buddy drop back. What happened? Did he hit a slick spot? Will wondered. Yes!

"I've got you now, loser!" Will shouted.

"You've got Buddy . . . but who's got you?" a teasing female voice asked.

"Huh?" Will cried. He jerked his head around and stared into the backseat.

Empty.

He stared forward again and fought to keep the Cataluna under control around a curve.

"Well, well, well, William . . . this certainly is cozy.

I know you've been hunting for me. And here we are—together," the girl's voice purred.

"What's happening here?" Will cried. "Who are you?"

The wheel bounced under his hands. He struggled to keep the speeding car in control.

"I used to know someone named Will—William—many years ago. Many, many, years ago." The girl's voice filled the car. Filled Will's head.

"What is this? Some kind of joke?"

The Cataluna swung crazily into the next turn, an S-shaped curve. Will jerked the wheel hard, straightening the car out.

"Don't play innocent with me, Will Parker. It's your old friend Catherine."

Will glanced at the side mirror. The Chevelle was now only inches behind. "Shut up!" he shouted. "Shut up! I'm not losing this race over a stupid joke!"

Will pumped the brake as he hit the middle of the S-curve. Then he put on the gas for the second turn.

"You are not fooling anyone, pretending you are interested in this race." The girl laughed. *"I recognized you right away. Too bad our reunion has to be so short."*

Stay calm, Will told himself. Stay calm. Get ready for the curve.

He tried to turn the wheel. It stuck. It wouldn't move.

He jerked on the stick shift. Frozen.

"Try the brake, Will," cooed the voice. *"Go on. Maybe it will work. Go on—try."*

Will slammed on the brake pedal.

The car sped faster.

Will uttered a harsh scream of terror.

"Oh, thank you, Mr. Parker!" the voice cried happily. *"Thank you! I enjoyed that!"*

Will slammed on the brake pedal again. Again. He saw Buddy pull up beside the Cataluna.

Will pounded on the window. "Help!" he screamed. But Buddy didn't see him. His eyes were focused on the road.

"As you know . . . all good things must come to an end." The girl laughed, cruel laughter.

William hit the short straight run along the cliffs. "Leave me alone!" he shrieked. "I don't know you. I don't know you!"

"Goodbye, William!" the girl cried.

The Cataluna lurched to the right. It smashed hard into Buddy's car.

Will fought to turn the wheel as the Cataluna spun wildly across the road. He tipped sideways. "Noooo!" Will shrieked as the car tilted over the cliffside.

Will's head banged against the side window. Everything went black.

He heard shattering glass. And the groan of bending metal.

Pain shot through his body. He tasted blood in his mouth. His arm was trapped against the door. It throbbed with every heartbeat. Broken, he thought.

Will forced himself to open his eyes, blinking until he could focus.

He stared out the windshield. Afraid to move. Almost afraid to breathe.

But he didn't go tumbling down the cliffside. The Cataluna's front bumper had snagged on the cliff face.

Will peered down the road. He saw the Chevelle roll over completely, landing back on its tires.

"Oh, wow. Buddy's trapped in there."

The Chevelle rocked for a moment.

Then exploded.

chapter

15

"*H*ey—!"

Buddy uttered a startled cry as the Cataluna bumped hard against the passenger side of the Chevelle.

The Chevelle bounced into the cliffside. Metal scraped against stone.

Buddy's head slammed into the ceiling. The wheel bounced out from under his grasp.

The car bounced off the cliff wall, back into the road.

Buddy spun the wheel, struggling to regain control.

Another shriek of metal as his door scraped the cliffside again.

Then the door flew open.

"Heeeeeyy—!" Buddy's cry rose up over the roar of the engine as he was tossed out of the car.

He hit the pavement on his side. Pain burned through his entire body. Crippling pain.

He rolled over once. Twice. His head hit the pavement. He rolled until he came to a stop in the middle of the road.

He shut his eyes as the explosion made the ground shake. Lying on his stomach, pain raging up and down his body, he heard the explosion, so close, so close. He felt a blast of hot air, heard shattering glass, the roar of flames.

"Will—!" he cried.

Thick smoke choked his throat. He pulled himself to his knees, struggling to breathe, struggling to see.

"Will!"

He turned his gaze up the road. No sign of Will or the Cataluna.

With a pained cry he turned back. And saw the burning Chevelle, flames pouring out of the windows and out the open door. And the Cataluna a few yards behind it on the cliff edge.

Buddy took a deep breath, tasting smoke in his mouth. Then, using all of his remaining strength, he shoved himself back to his feet and staggered toward the Cataluna.

"Not a scratch," he mumbled. "Not a scratch on that evil car."

Buddy heard the roar of cars racing toward him on River Road.

It's my friends, he realized, his vision still fuzzy, his head throbbing. They're coming to find out who won.

He saw that the Chevelle had skidded farther down the road than the Cataluna. "I guess I won," he muttered, half-dazed, struggling to force away the pain.

Before he could stop it, a shrill laugh escaped his throat.

I'm alive! he thought, as if just realizing it. I don't believe it. I'm alive!

He heard cars screech to a stop behind him. He heard horrified shouts. Alarmed cries.

Buddy didn't care about the other kids. He and Will made it. Nothing else mattered. They were alive!

Buddy grabbed the door handle to the Cataluna and swung the door open.

"Come on, man. I got you."

A long cut slanted across Will's forehead. Blood matted Will's blond hair to his forehead.

The cut only seems bad, Buddy told himself, squinting into the car. Face cuts are bad bleeders.

"Come on—give me a hand here, Will," Buddy called. "Let's get you out . . . make sure you're okay."

Will did not answer.

Buddy heard the thud of shoes on the pavement. His friends coming to help.

"Will—come on, man. Come on," Buddy urged. "You're okay, aren't you? You're okay—right? Right!"

Will did not answer.

Another laugh escaped Buddy's throat. Crazy, hysterical laughter. "Guess I really am the winner, right, Will?"

Tears streamed down Buddy's face. He laughed until he choked.

"Yes, I'm the winner. Because you're dead, Will!" Buddy couldn't tell if he was laughing or crying. "Because you're dead."

chapter

16

"*G*oodbye, William. And good riddance."

Feelings of joy and triumph swept over Catherine. Even trapped inside the steel and glass body of the car, her spirit nearly burst with happiness. And relief.

"You will never take your revenge. I will never again have to worry about you following me, tracking me, pursuing me."

William Parker failed.

In his new body, new clothes, with his shortened name, he failed.

Catherine of the Bad Moon triumphed. He died in her grasp.

Now she wanted to celebrate. She wanted to raise

her head and howl up at the moon and stars. She wanted to run barefoot through the dark, fragrant woods. She wanted to splash through the river below, feel the cold water against her skin.

But she had no skin. No freedom to run.

She was trapped inside steel and chrome. Trapped forever.

"More people will pay for my sorrow," she told herself. *"More people will pay with their lives for my unhappy fate."*

William Parker was gone. Dead and defeated.

But Catherine could not celebrate for long.

She hated those whose spirits were free, hated all who could walk free and talk—and *live.*

And she would make them pay.

Buddy grabbed Will under the armpits. Got to get him out of the car, he thought.

The toe of one of Will's boots caught on the door handle. Buddy yanked hard. "Come on. Come on," Buddy murmured, feeling hot tears on his cheeks. "You can't stay in there, Will. This car is evil."

The faint wail of a siren invaded Buddy's frantic, swirling thoughts. He glanced behind him to find a cluster of kids staring in horror at him.

He gave Will's body another jerk. I don't care if he's dead. He shouldn't be in there. No one is getting in the Cataluna again. No one. Ever.

"Buddy," someone called softly.

He turned. Sara knelt beside him, her blond hair down over her face. Her chin trembling.

Buddy tugged on Will's body again.

"Buddy, what are you doing?" Sara asked gently.

Buddy turned to her, blinking rapidly, trying to clear his vision, clear the thick smoke swirls from his mind.

"What are you doing?" she repeated.

"I don't know," Buddy admitted. "I want to get Will out of the car."

"But he's dead, Buddy. Let go of him. Wait for the police. He's dead."

"No. I have to get him out. I have to."

Sara sighed. "Are you okay?"

"I—I don't know."

She climbed to her feet behind him, brushing her hair back. "Let me help you." Sara leaned into the car and released Will's boot from the door handle.

Buddy slid him out and lay him on the ground. He crouched down beside Will. "I'm sorry," he whispered. He smoothed his hand over Will's eyes, closing them.

He felt Sara's hand on his shoulder. He stood slowly, every movement painful. Holding on to him, Sara led Buddy away from the car—away from Will's body.

The kids in the crowd hung back, silent, frightened. "You're shaking," Sara said. She wrapped her arms around him. "I'm sorry, Buddy. So sorry about everything. I've been so stupid."

Buddy pulled Sara closer to him. "It's okay," he murmured.

"No, it isn't." She pressed her cheek against his. "I don't know what's wrong with me. The way I've been acting lately. It isn't like me. I—I can't explain it. . . ." Her voice trailed off.

It's the car, Buddy wanted to tell her. It's the Cataluna, that evil car. It got to us both.

But he knew she wouldn't understand. He knew she wouldn't believe him.

"It's okay," he said again. "It's all okay. It's over now."

"Hey—the police!" someone yelled.

Buddy didn't move. He heard people running. Cars starting.

Buddy didn't know what he could tell the police. But he wasn't going to run away.

Sara stared up at him.

"Go," he urged her. "The police don't have to know you were here."

"No, I'm staying," Sara replied firmly. She held on to his arm. "I'm staying with you."

"But, Sara—"

To his surprise, Buddy saw a dark-haired girl running across the pavement toward them. Marisol!

"Marisol—go home!" he cried, waving his arms frantically. "You don't want to be involved. Get away—fast!"

He uttered a startled cry as Marisol ran past without slowing, without glancing at him.

"Where is she going?" Sara cried.

"Marisol—! Hey—!" Buddy called to her.

He didn't realize that Marisol was running to the Cataluna until he saw her grab the door handle and pull the door open.

"Hey—stop!" he cried. He pulled free of Sara and lurched toward the car. "Marisol—get away from there! Marisol—are you crazy?"

chapter

17

Marisol pulled the door shut. She saw Buddy running toward her. But she knew he'd never catch her now.

She backed up the car, then floored the gas. The car pulled forward with a roar. Yes! she thought. At last!

She pulled the wheel hard to the left, swinging the Cataluna out onto the dogleg overlooking the river.

A girl's voice suddenly filled the car: *"And what do you think you're doing?"*

Marisol didn't cry out in surprise. Instead, she smiled.

"I asked what you thought you were doing!" The voice demanded angrily.

Marisol's smile didn't fade.

116

"I'm stealing you, Catherine," she replied. "I'm putting an end to your evil once and for all."

Marisol downshifted as the car rounded a curve, climbing through the darkness above the river. Then she lowered her foot on the gas pedal.

"Wouldn't you say I've learned a little since the last time we met—Bad Luck Catherine?" Marisol said, her dark eyes flashing with excitement.

The sound of a strangled gasp filled the car.

"Yes," Marisol said, eyes straight ahead on the curving, twisting River Road. "I don't blame you for not recognizing me, Catherine. But it is me inside this girl's body. It is me—your old friend William Parker."

"No!" the voice shrieked. *"I killed you, William! I just killed you!"*

"No, Catherine. You killed another innocent," Marisol replied softly. "That boy Will was just a boy. A boy eager to drive a sleek, fast car. But he had no knowledge of you or your three-hundred-year-old evil."

Leaning over the wheel, William knew the real fight would soon begin. And he couldn't wait. He couldn't wait to destroy Catherine Hatchett—Cataluna— forever. He couldn't wait to avenge his father and his brother.

And Stan McCloy, William added, thinking of Buddy. And all the victims of Bad Luck Catherine.

"Now you are through, Catherine!" William

shouted in Marisol's voice. "Now this ends. It finally ends!"

Catherine uttered a cruel laugh. *"You cannot stop me,"* she replied confidently. *"Don't you know that by now, William? You try and try, but you cannot."* Her laughter filled the car.

William concentrated on the road and didn't reply. He struggled to control his excitement. He had waited centuries for this moment. He was determined not to fail now.

"Remember Jessica Mason?" Catherine taunted. *"You killed her, William Parker. In your attempt to end my life, you killed an innocent girl. Who will you kill this time?"*

William's stomach twisted as he remembered driving the knife into poor, innocent Jessica. Don't listen, he ordered himself. Don't listen. You must be strong. This time you will triumph. This time you will stop Catherine's evil.

Dark trees whirred past in a blur as the car sped forward, up the deserted road. William hunched over the wheel, thinking hard.

Distract her, he reminded himself. If your plan is to work, you must distract her.

"I kept after you, Catherine," William told her. "It took me so long to find you in this time—in this form. In the crash I had been transformed into a teenage girl. I expected to find you in a human form as well."

William suddenly felt Catherine trying to gain

control of the car. Beneath his hands, he felt tension building in the steering wheel.

"In the end you were easy to find," William continued. "I watched for death and destruction. When I found a photograph of the Doom Car—and saw the red crescent moon on the fender—I knew."

William felt the gas pedal and the clutch stiffen beneath his feet. No. I can't lose control now, he thought. I need more time. More time.

"I never gave up the search for you, Bad Luck Catherine. Never. Not once. And now . . . now I've finally got you!"

A low grinding sound tore through the car. Metal scraped against metal.

William gripped the wheel so tightly his hands ached. What is she doing? What is Catherine going to try?

"It's too bad you found me, William. You should have spent your life as Marisol!" Catherine called triumphantly.

The Cataluna began to shake.

"You should have stayed away, William."

The car's horn blared. The wipers beat back and forth across the windshield. The cigarette lighter glowed in the dashboard.

She almost has full control, William realized. Not much time left.

"Oh, yes!" Catherine screamed. *"You've found me, William. And I am so happy you did!"*

119

The front seat bucked. William's chest hurtled into the steering wheel.

Pain shot through his body. He felt as if his lungs were about to explode.

Don't let go, he ordered himself, struggling to breathe. Do not let go!

"Now I'll have the pleasure of killing you all over again!" Catherine's laughter echoed through the car.

William's hands shot up as the steering wheel began to spin. A howl of horror escaped his throat as the car whirled wildly out of control.

Off the road. A hard bump. Then another that sent his head smashing against the windshield.

The car bucked. Then bounced hard, bouncing William inside like a helpless crash dummy.

Get control, he ordered himself. Grab the wheel. Grab it back. Get control.

But Catherine was in control now.

"This time you die forever—William. Forever!"

The Cataluna sailed off the edge of the cliff.

It soared into the darkness.

Then began to fall.

chapter

18

The Cataluna slammed over the cliffside. William threw his arms over his face.

He felt the car drop.

It flipped onto its roof.

He squeezed his eyes shut and began to pray.

The car plunged straight down—and landed with a hard crash on the road beside the river.

William felt as though he were still plunging down. Dizzy, he thought. So dizzy. He couldn't hear—his ears ringing. Bright dots of light darted before his eyes.

He lifted his head. A sharp, sour taste rose in his throat.

But I am alive, he realized. Still alive. And of course the car wasn't damaged at all.

You must destroy Catherine, he ordered himself, forcing himself alert.

I can't, he thought. He let his head drop back. I can't. I can't. I can't.

William closed his eyes. Blackness surrounded him. He sank into it, thoughts of Catherine drifting away.

Images flashed through William's mind. He saw himself as Marisol, eating doughnuts with Buddy. Then he saw himself three hundred years earlier. Riding his pony as a little boy in the West Hampshire Colony. Standing in his mother's kitchen, licking batter off a spoon. Wrestling with his brother, Joseph, their father laughing as he watched.

Father and Joseph. William shivered. Don't think about them, he told himself.

He tried to return to the pleasant visions. Anything to escape the pain.

But he could not stop the dark images from coming. He saw Catherine in the form of a cat. She leaped at his brother, claws out.

Her claws ripped through Joseph's eyes. William heard Joseph's scream of agony. Once again he saw Joseph's shattered eyeballs lying on the ground.

The images swirled and changed. William grew colder.

He watched Catherine take on a new shape. A rat. A white rat.

The rat dived into his father's mouth. Her long tail hanging from between his lips. William saw his father's face grow red. Heard his father choke, unable to breathe. Suffocating.

The memories forced William to open his eyes. She killed my brother and my father. I must stop her, William thought. I must.

He stared out the car window. The car had landed right side up on the dogleg curve of road running along the river.

William knew what he must do.

Taking a deep breath, he lowered his foot on the gas pedal. "You lose, Cataluna. This time you lose! You will never kill again!"

A few seconds later the car pulled forward, as if it hadn't plunged down a steep cliff.

William glanced at the speedometer.

Sixty.

Faster. Have to go faster. He didn't know how long he could keep control of the Cataluna.

He stomped on the gas, demanding more power.

"What are you doing?" Catherine shrieked.

"Preparing to destroy you!" William shouted back.

Catherine did not reply.

What is she plotting now? William wondered.

The curves came faster and faster. The road grew slippery, slick with a heavy, late-night dew.

William glanced at the speedometer.

Seventy.

Talk to Catherine, he urged himself. Keep her busy. This is your last chance. Your very last chance, William. Take it. Use it.

"Shall I tell you how I plan to destroy you?" William called.

Catherine remained silent.

Does she have a plan of her own? William thought. Is that why she doesn't answer?

"Your own mother condemned you, Bad Luck Catherine!" William cried.

Catherine did not reply.

"Yes," William continued. "Your own mother showed me how to kill you. Aren't you curious, Catherine? Don't you want to know the one thing that can destroy you?"

"You don't frighten me," Catherine replied uncertainly.

But she does sound frightened, William heard. Good. Maybe she doesn't have a plan after all.

His eyes darted to the speedometer.

Eighty.

Not too much longer, he thought. Then I will make my move.

"Many, many years ago when I was searching for you in the West Hampshire Colony, I went back to your mother's little house in the woods. . . ."

William paused, grabbing a quick peek at the speedometer.

Eighty-five.

"I hoped I would find you. I searched the cabin.

124

Tore it apart. Do you know what I found, Catherine?" William narrowed his eyes on the road. "I found a letter. A letter your mother wrote to you. The letter explained how the Cataluna works. I'm so glad I found the letter before you did."

The white car skidded on a curve. It slammed into the cliff. Rocks pelted the hood and windshield.

William pressed down on the gas.

"That letter explained everything about the car, Catherine. Everything. Of course, I didn't understand one word of it at the time. To a poor fool from 1698 it didn't make much sense."

William glanced at the dashboard.

Ninety.

Hold on a little longer, he told himself. You only get one try.

"But I understand now," he announced. "I understand everything!"

Up ahead William spotted a break in the curves. A stretch of straight road stretching into the darkness along the river.

Perfect, he thought.

But the car skidded as he whipped around the last turn. It spun toward the embankment.

"No!" William uttered a cry as he struggled with the wheel. He knew the car would plunge into the river if he didn't control it.

He twisted the wheel again. The car straightened out.

Yes! he thought.

William jammed the gas pedal to the floor.

"Yes, Catherine. I understand everything!" William cried.

Ninety-five.

One hundred. One hundred miles per hour.

Now! William thought.

He jerked the Cataluna's gearshift into reverse.

"Nooooo!" Catherine shrieked. *"Noooooo! You can't do this! You can't! What is happening to me? What have you done?"*

An ear-piercing shriek filled the car, louder than the squealing tires beneath them.

The Cataluna spun wildly. William spun with it, whirling as if inside a dark tornado. Were they still on the road? In the air? In the river? He couldn't tell.

William's skin sizzled. His eyes felt as if they wanted to bulge out of his head. His entire body felt about to explode.

The car spun faster, whirring, roaring, squealing into a well of deep darkness.

chapter

___

19

William landed on something soft and smooth—and motionless. A pleasant warmth spread over his body.

Where am I? he wondered. Am I alive? Have I died again?

He sat up slowly, carefully. Gazed around. And found himself in the backseat of the Cataluna.

Has it worked? he wondered. Has my plan worked?

Bright sunlight beamed into the car. No longer midnight anymore, William realized.

The Cataluna stood in a small clearing surrounded by forest.

Am I home? William wondered. Am I really home?

He glanced down. I have my old body back. I'm me again. Not Marisol.

So that means that Catherine . . .

William peered over into the front seat. Catherine lay sprawled in the seat. A girl again.

So small, William thought. A young girl. How could she have killed so many people?

Catherine groaned and sat up. She turned and stared over the seat back at him. "You're back in your own—" She grabbed the rearview mirror and jerked it down. Catherine ran her hands over her face. She touched her hair. "It is!" she cried. "It *is* me!"

William reached for the door handle.

"What have you done?" Catherine asked.

"I've taken us for a ride," he told her. He eased himself out of the car. Pain shot through his body.

He tilted back his head and closed his eyes. The sun shone down on his face, allowing it to warm him, to soothe him.

William heard a car door slam behind him.

No time to enjoy yourself now, he reminded himself. Your plan is only half complete.

He turned to face Catherine. Stall her, he thought. Don't let her get away. Talk to her. Don't let her guess your plan.

"I brought us home, Catherine," William told her. "If what your mother wrote in that letter is correct, we should be back where we started. Back in 1698. In the West Hampshire Colony."

Catherine studied the clearing. She gazed from the

car to the little house. The house where her mother had lived.

William moved around the car toward her. "And now, Catherine," he declared, "I am going to put an end to your evil forever!"

He expected Catherine to try to escape. But she stared back at him calmly.

Then she threw her head back and laughed.

Doesn't she realize that she is no longer indestructible? William wondered. As a car, she could sustain any injury. But now she is human again.

A human who can bleed. A human whose bones can break. A human who can die.

A human who can be killed.

"Oh, William," Catherine said, her expression turning serious. "If only all the Parkers were as stupid as you. None of this would have happened."

Stay calm, he warned himself. Don't get distracted. "What are you talking about?" he demanded.

"Poor William." Catherine shook her head. "You worked so long . . . tried so hard. And all for nothing."

William stared at Catherine.

He watched her begin to change. To shrink. To grow thick, gray fur.

A rat. She's turning into a rat, William saw. No. I can't let her get away. He dived for her.

Missed.

The gray rat, its pink tail whipping behind it, disappeared in the knee-high grass.

"No!" William shouted. "No! You will not escape me this time!"

He dropped to his knees and trailed her through the grass.

Up ahead, he heard a soft skittering noise. The grass shifted.

Careful, he told himself. Careful. No sudden movements. No sound.

William gently pushed apart the blades of grass. He saw a flash of gray fur.

You've almost got her, he thought. Almost got her.

William bent lower.

Catherine sprang.

She leaped onto his shoulder and stuck her head into his ear. William screamed as her small, sharp teeth dug into the tender skin of his cheek.

William grabbed frantically at the rat. Clenched his fist. Tried to choke the animal.

Catherine squirmed in his grasp—and wriggled into his shirtsleeve.

William felt Catherine's rat feet scurry up his arm. He shook his arm.

Too late.

She popped out of his collar and sprang onto his face.

With a hideous screech, she reached out both claws and began to rake his face to shreds.

chapter

20

"Noooo!"

Howling in pain, William grabbed at the rat—and batted it to the ground.

It landed on its back in the dirt with a soft *thud*.

Ignoring the blood that trickled down his cheeks, he dived after the rat and captured it in one hand.

"You are not getting away this time," he declared breathlessly, squeezing the rat until it squeaked.

He raised the rat in front of his face. He glared at it, squinting through the blood running into his eyes. Then he swung his hand down, smashing the rat into the ground.

"That should hold you!" he cried. The rat went limp in his hand.

He staggered back to the little house at the edge of the clearing, the house that had belonged to Catherine's mother.

"Welcome home," he murmured to the rat.

It uttered a shrill squeak, and William could feel it trying to escape again.

He crossed to a table in the corner and found a battered wire cage. He stuffed the rat inside and snapped the rusty latch closed.

The scratches on William's face burned and throbbed. His head ached.

Almost finished, William told himself. Almost finished. Then you can rest.

"Now you come with me," he said to the rat. He picked up the cage. "I don't want you to miss any of this. You deserve to see it all."

He carried the cage outside and set it down on the tiny porch. He could hear the rat's claws scraping against the metal.

"I am sure I will find what I need behind the house," he told Catherine. "You wait here."

The rat's black eyes burned with hatred.

"Now we're getting to the fun part," William told himself. He hurried around the corner of the house.

"I knew it!" he cried. "This is perfect."

He strained to lift the weathered old ax. Resting it on his shoulder, he made his way back to Catherine. When he showed her the ax, he thought he saw a shiver run through her body.

"Watch carefully, now." He raised the ax over the cage that held Catherine prisoner.

Then he turned and headed to the Cataluna. A fierce cry escaped his throat as he brought the ax down on the windshield. The glass cracked—and shattered.

"Do you understand what I'm doing, Catherine?" he called breathlessly.

He brought the ax down hard on the sideview mirror. The mirror fell to the ground, bounced once, then disappeared into the tall grass.

With each crack of the ax the rat let out a furious screech.

William aimed the ax at the Cataluna's hood. He brought it down with a loud groan. The blade sliced through the glossy white finish. The ax landed on the hood again. Again.

The frantic rat leaped up against the cage, screeching its anger.

The fourth blow broke the hood lock. The hood sprang open, revealing the engine.

"Your mother came from the twentieth century, Catherine." William's breath came harsh and ragged.

He raised the ax again, grunting. He sliced down through the engine.

His arms trembled. His heart thudded in his chest. Keep going, he urged himself. It is almost over. Finish and you destroy Catherine forever.

"Your mother came from the twentieth century.

She came to the West Hampshire Colony—to the year 1698. She traveled back in time in this car."

He swung the ax down on the engine again. The car bounced from the blow. The engine cracked.

"You were born here in the sixteen-hundreds!" he shouted to the rat. "But this car was built in the future. In the twentieth century."

He glanced at the cage on the ground. The rat heaved itself against the door, clawing and screeching in protest.

"I'm going to destroy the car now," William explained, breathing hard. "Now. In 1698. I'm going to destroy the car three hundred years before it was built."

He turned and swung the ax again at the engine. The blow fell short, shattering one of the headlights. The sound of cracking glass echoed through the silent forest.

Catherine clawed desperately at the cage, throwing herself against the door, squirming to reach the rusty latch.

William swung the ax again. Again.

"I'm destroying this car nearly three hundred years before your mother was born, Catherine!" he cried over the sound of his ax blows. "Do you know what that means? That means your mother will never exist in this time and place. And so, *you* will never exist. You *will never be born!*"

"Nooooooo!"

William heard Catherine's desperate, terrified cry through the glass. The rat flung its body against the side of the cage. The cage fell onto its side in the grass.

"You will never be born, Catherine!" William shouted, swinging the ax again. "You and your evil will never be born. And my family will live in peace. My father and brother will not die by your hand. You will not exist. Not exist."

William swung the ax in rhythm with his words.

"Not exist. Not exist."

He heard another long howl of protest from Catherine. Louder this time. Closer.

With a gasp of surprise, he turned away from the battered car. And saw the cage on its side.

The door open.

The rat scampering over the grass. Sprouting gray wings. Flapping thin gray wings. The wings crackling in the air as Catherine rose.

Rose above William.

Transformed into a bat now. Red eyes aflame, burning into William's eyes. Wings flapping. Pointed teeth curling out over black lips.

"Unh—" William managed a frightened groan. He raised the ax.

The bat hovered over him.

Red eyes glowing, Catherine uttered a hiss of fury. "You're dead, William!" she cried.

She swooped down, down, so fast William couldn't see her, couldn't move.

Down she swooped, the gray wings buzzing like an engine.

Down. Down. Red eyes a blazing streak of fire.

Opening her ugly mouth in a shrill scream. And then burying long, curled teeth into William's throat.

chapter

21

As the bat sank its fangs into William's neck, he staggered back. Fell against the battered hood of the car.

He let out a howl of pain. The ax dropped from his hand.

He reached up with both hands and tried to grab the buzzing wings, tried to tear the creature away.

But Catherine held on, sinking her teeth deeper.

William felt the warm blood flow down his neck. Felt wave after wave of pain shoot down his body.

I can't weaken now, he told himself. I'm so close. I cannot let her defeat me now.

He tumbled off the car and bent to pick up the ax.

The bat uttered a shrill screech as its fangs dug

deeper into William's throat. The dry wings scratched against his neck. He smelled the creature's sour breath in his face.

Shutting his eyes, William tried to ignore the pain.

He raised the ax, heavy now, so much heavier. He gripped the handle in both hands.

Swung hard.

The engine cracked again and fell to the ground.

William swung hard, slicing a fender off the car.

The bat uttered a furious screech. Its wings buzzed harder. The curled fangs drilled deeper.

"Ohhhh," William moaned as he raised the heavy ax again.

He sliced the axle in two. The car toppled forward, the front dropping to the grass as if wounded.

Fatally wounded?

William raised the ax.

So heavy. So heavy. Too heavy.

It fell from his hand.

The pain roared through his body. The teeth cut into his throat. He could feel the steady throb of the blood as it poured out.

Poured out. Flowed out.

He felt his strength flowing out with it. Felt his strength pouring out onto the red-stained grass.

So weak now. So weak he could no longer stand.

The bat screeched its shrill anger, flapped its gray wings, its head buried in his neck.

So weak. All of his strength pouring out, pouring . . . pouring . . .

William fell to his knees.

He shut his eyes against the pain. But still it throbbed from his throat. From the deep wound in his throat.

"Oh, help me," he choked out as he fell forward onto the grass. Facedown.

His body shuddered as the bat released him from its grip.

His body shuddered again as Catherine flew up over him, batting her wings, bright scarlet blood dripping from her black bat lips, from her curved, yellow fangs.

Then William didn't move.

"I have won!" Catherine declared in a shriek of joy. "Die in torment, William!"

chapter

22

I swooped over William, enjoying my victory.

I darted high in the afternoon sky, high above the green trees of the forest surrounding West Hampshire. I spread my wings and floated, feeling the warm wind, feeling the sunlight, feeling so much joy.

I was free.

Free from that steel and glass body I had been trapped in for so long in that future world. Free to fly. Free to soar.

And free of William Parker.

Free of his anger, of his hatred. Free of his unending desire to destroy me.

Still tasting his blood in my mouth, so sweet, so

tantalizingly sweet, I soared above him. Then swooped low again, my eyes enjoying the sight of his sprawled, unmoving body. So pale.

So lifeless.

How long did I float there enjoying my triumph?

I don't really know. But eventually I sank back to earth, screeching out my happiness.

And began to change myself. To change myself back to my human form. Back to Catherine.

How I longed to be a girl again. How I longed to brush my hair, to wear a long skirt, to walk barefoot in the sweet, fragrant grass.

I drew in my bat wings. I stretched myself . . . stretched.

I became Catherine once again.

And remembered that the village elders would not allow me to walk barefoot in the grass. The village elders—those hateful men—had declared me bad luck.

Bad Luck Catherine. Born under a bad moon.

Well, fine, I decided. I am back now. I will be bad luck if they wish it. Back luck for them.

I turned to the trees, trying to figure out the direction. The afternoon sun floated high in the clear sky.

I glanced at the battered car. The Cataluna, now shattered and broken.

And saw someone move inside it.

Someone in the front seat.

Someone stepped out of the broken door. A human figure. A young man.

Startled, I shielded my eyes with one hand, trying to recognize him.

Who could it be? Who could be in that wrecked and ruined shell of a car?

"No!"

I cried out when I recognized him.

Stan. Stan McCloy.

He floated out from the car, eyes wide, his gaze so blank, so blank and lifeless. Floated over the grass, no expression on his face, his face as blank as his stare.

"No!" I cried. "You're dead! You're dead!"

I took a step back as I saw another figure float out from the car. A figure clothed in black. Shielding my eyes from the bright sunlight, I struggled to see him clearly.

I saw blond hair. I saw the same blank expression.

I recognized the long black jacket. I recognized the boy named Will, the boy I had mistaken for William Parker.

"No! You're dead, too!" My frightened cry.

He followed Stan McCloy, floating over the grass, floating so silently toward me.

And then I saw the others. Floating up from the car. I didn't remember their names. But I remembered their faces.

The faces of the dead.

The people who had died in the Cataluna.

Blank faces. Blank eyes, all trained on me as one by one they stepped silently from the car.

"You're dead! You're dead! You're all dead!" My shrill cry echoing through the still forest trees.

The faces all floating together now. Floating from the car where they had died.

The faces all staring at me, glaring at me. So solemn, so . . . inhumanly solemn.

So dead.

Before I could run, before I could change my form and escape, they had wrapped around me in a wide circle. Their eyes on me, unblinking, so stern and unforgiving, they surrounded me.

And began to spin.

A circle of angry faces, a circle of the dead.

All of the victims of the Cataluna. All of *my* victims.

Back in time. Back to stare at me, to circle me.

To spin around me.

Faster now. Spinning faster until the faces blurred. And the dead faces became one staring, dead face.

Spinning into a dark blur. The whirling figures spinning so fast, spinning out the sunlight, shutting out all light, until all I could see were the staring eyes, the angry staring eyes in the blank, dead, whirling faces.

Circling me. Circling and drawing in tighter, closer, closer as they spun, until I saw the sky go black and felt the ground tremble beneath me.

And then beyond the whirring circle of dead faces, I

heard a faint cry. A voice I recognized at once. William Parker's voice.

"I have defeated you, Catherine."

Those were the words I heard him call. William Parker. Still alive. Outside the circle of faces. Outside the circle of victims.

And I knew he told the truth.

I knew that I was the victim now.

"I have defeated you, Catherine," he called to me from beyond the curtain of the dead. "I have destroyed the car. Your victims will all live. They will all return to their time and live their lives as they should."

And then William's voice was drowned out by the roar of spinning faces, spinning into a dark blur, tightening the circle, tightening it.

Pulling me. Pulling me in all directions.

Until I could no longer scream. No longer breathe.

I felt my body, my human body, my girl's body, tear apart.

Tear into pieces. Tiny, tiny pieces. Millions of tiny pieces. All of them Catherine. All of them spinning in darkness now, spinning with the dead. Spinning forever.

And so William had his victory.

He won his revenge.

And on that day, I died.

In fact . . . I never lived.

epilogue

William groaned and pulled himself up onto his elbows. He opened his eyes, surprised to find himself on the grass, in the forest.

He lifted his gaze to the sky and saw the afternoon sun high over the trees.

His throat tingled. He rubbed it gently. A mosquito bite, probably.

But what am I doing out here in the middle of the day? he wondered.

He took a deep breath, then pulled himself to his feet. His eyes followed a brown rabbit hopping through the tall grass. As he was about to turn away, he saw two figures running out from the trees.

Two men dressed in black. Running harder now

that they had seen him. Both waving their arms at him.

"William!" one of them called.

Squinting against the sunlight, William recognized them both. "Father!" he shouted happily. "Joseph!"

Yes. His father and brother, waving happily as they moved toward him over the tall forest grass.

His heart pounding, he ran to meet them.

Why do I feel as if I have not seen them for a long while? he wondered. Why do I have the feeling I have been away?

He couldn't answer the questions. He only knew that seeing them both now filled him with joy.

"William, why are you out here in the forest?" his father demanded.

"We have been searching the colony for you," his brother Joseph declared breathlessly.

"Are you feeling well?" his father asked, his blue eyes studying William's pale face. "Your eyes do not look clear, son."

"I—I think I fell asleep out here," William stammered.

"Well, let us not waste the day in this clearing." Joseph tugged impatiently on William's shirtsleeve. "We have been searching for you because we have exciting news."

William allowed Joseph to pull him toward the village. Their father hurried to keep up.

"Tell me the news at once," William demanded, beginning to feel his energy restored.

"You have a new sister," his father revealed, a broad smile creasing his normally somber face.

"How wonderful!" William cried.

"Mother had her baby and is doing well," Joseph told him happily. "We have a new little sister, William. Come see."

What a happy day, William thought, following them through the town to their cottage. No wonder the sun is shining so brightly today. I have a new baby sister.

Stepping inside, he waited for his eyes to adjust to the dark room. He found his mother sitting by the hearth, gently rocking a small wooden cradle.

"Let me see her!" he eagerly exclaimed.

He leaned over the cradle and stared down at the sleeping baby, tightly swaddled in a white blanket.

"She's so small and delicate," William declared.

He gazed down happily at her tiny pink hands. His eyes moved up her tiny body, wrapped so tightly in the swaddling blanket.

He admired her silky blond hair. She slept so soundly, so peacefully.

Then, with a little sigh, she turned her head.

William squinted hard when he saw the little red spot on her temple.

What *was* that?

A tiny red crescent moon?

About the Author

"Where do you get your ideas?"

That's the question that R. L. Stine is asked most often. "I don't know where my ideas come from," he says. "But I do know that I have a lot more scary stories in my mind that I can't wait to write."

So far, he has written more than fifty mysteries and thrillers for young people, all of them bestsellers.

Bob grew up in Columbus, Ohio. Today he lives in an apartment near Central Park in New York City with his wife, Jane, and fourteen-year-old son, Matt.

THE NIGHTMARES
NEVER END . . .
WHEN YOU VISIT

Next . .
THE STEPSISTER 2
(Coming mid-October 1995)

Emily Case knows she should be happy her sister
Nancy is coming home from the mental hospital.
Everyone tells her Nancy is completely cured. But
what if they are wrong? What if Nancy tries to kill
her—the way she did last year?

A few days after Nancy's return, Emily finds her
favorite dress cut in half. Is Nancy up to her old
tricks? Is she going to try to kill Emily again? Or does
someone else have plans to hurt Emily?

R·L·STINE

presents

THE
FEAR STREET®
1996 CALENDAR

Spend 1996 on
FEAR STREET

Vampires, evil cheerleaders, ghosts, and all the boys and ghouls of R. L. Stine's Fear Street books are here to help you shriek through the seasons. It's the perfect way to keep track of your days, nights, and nightmares....

Special Bonus Poster

A map of Shadyside showing where all the horrors of Fear Street happened. Take a terrifying tour of the spots where your favorite characters lived—and died.

Coming soon

1098
A Fear Street Calendar/Published by Archway Paperbacks